SPOILED ROTTEN

SPOILED ROTTEN

A Liz Walker Mystery

Mary Jackman

DUNDURN
TORONTO

Editor: Shannon Whibbs
Design: Courtney Horner
Printer: Webcom

Library and Archives Canada Cataloguing in Publication

Jackman, Mary (Mary Elizabeth)
   Spoiled rotten : a Liz Walker mystery / Mary Jackman.

Issued also in electronic formats.
ISBN 978-1-4597-0141-0

   I. Title.

PS8619.A227S66 2012   C813'.6   C2011-906003-5

1   2   3   4   5   16   15   14   13   12

  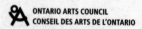

We acknowledge the support of the Canada Council for the Arts and the Ontario Arts Council for our publishing program. We also acknowledge the financial support of the Government of Canada through the Canada Book Fund and Livres Canada Books, and the Government of Ontario through the Ontario Book Publishing Tax Credit and the Ontario Media Development Corporation.

Care has been taken to trace the ownership of copyright material used in this book. The author and the publisher welcome any information enabling them to rectify any references or credits in subsequent editions.

J. Kirk Howard, President

Printed and bound in Canada.
www.dundurn.com

Dundurn
3 Church Street, Suite 500
Toronto, Ontario, Canada
M5E 1M2

Gazelle Book Services Limited
White Cross Mills
High Town, Lancaster, England
LA1 4XS

Dundurn
2250 Military Road
Tonawanda, NY
U.S.A. 14150

*Dedicated to Larry Guest, my business partner
and good friend for over thirty years*

chapter one

At 8:00 a.m. my day was well under way. I hated serving breakfast. There's not much money in it and the staff often quit. Sleep-deprived waiters argued about sections while all-night revellers and decamped tourists from the local hotels fought over the booths. The bartender was muttering under his breath, the chef was nowhere in sight, and the substitute line cook was "in the weeds." I only hoped if the Eggs Benny were runny enough that someone might come back for dinner to spend some real cash. An unlikely scenario if there ever was one.

The noise in the room was deafening. As I tilted my head toward the speakers to hear what was playing, a woman screamed at the top of her lungs.

"A MOUSE!" Everyone froze.

Soft jazz filled the silence, all heads turned, and a little grey mouse scampered around the dining room floor until Kitty, our cat, pounced out of nowhere and stuffed it in her mouth.

"CHEQUE!" shouted someone else from the crowd.

With lightning speed I sprinted around the end of the bar, swept up the duo with one hand, and, smiling reassuringly to everyone, strode confidently out the restaurant's front door. Hired on as vermin-controller, Kitty had become the queen of stealth, much more effective than the bucket of death, and not nearly as messy. She was a battle-scarred cat with patches of missing fur, half a tail, and a permanently bent ear that made the other ear look fully cocked as if she found human conversation absolutely titillating. When we reached the alley, I tapped her nose. The mouse cannon-balled to the ground and slithered down a hole. Kitty, however, punished me with a venomous glare and then sidled off at a forty-five degree angle, her tailless bum held high in the air.

One thing a wily restaurateur learns after fifteen years is when to make a run for it. Trusting that the staff would calm things down faster without my intervention, I headed for the side door of the century-old building where my second-floor office was located. I brushed past a panhandler counting change in the stairwell, and, ignoring an uncontrollable urge to give him all my money, dropped a buck in his hat instead.

I climbed the paint-worn stairs to a shadowy corridor with fifteen-foot ceilings and burned-out fixtures overhead. Fortunately for me and the nefarious creatures who roamed the building at all hours, the exit signs cast just enough light to guide the way. Promising to change the light bulbs the minute my suction cups arrived in the mail, I headed toward the heavy metal door covered in multiple locks at the end of the hall. I stepped inside. Two men looked at me. Then one of them leaned back in his chair and waved his hand in a grand gesture as if addressing a crowd.

"On behalf of the entire room, I'd like to be the first to say, 'Welcome!'" Richard Best was my general manager. I tended to ignore the "welcomes" because I got one every time I walked through the door. He possessed a goofy sense of humor tinged by genius and borderline insanity. I couldn't live without him.

When I first opened Walker's Way Bistro fifteen years ago, Rick applied for a job as a waiter. During the interview, I acknowledged the long history of degrees accredited from various top quality universities and asked if he was playing some kind of game.

"No game. I liked school and stayed as long as humanly possible."

"You have a Ph.D. in psychology."

"I had an office for six months and found out I didn't like talking to strangers about their problems."

"Some of our customers might have problems."

"I'll deal with it. Am I hired or not?"

He stared across the tabletop, deliberately trying to rankle, his intense blue eyes waiting for a reaction. I got the impression he was secretly diagnosing me and wondered what he'd make of my recurring naked-at-the-gas-pump dream. His knowledge of the human condition would be a handy tool to have as a waiter, not to mention as someone on my payroll. I hired him immediately.

Rick was perfect for the job and within weeks I promoted him to general manager. He was a natural as a host, able to size up a customer's mood with a single glance, which was an admirable gift to possess as a purveyor of fine food and alcohol. He knew when to keep his distance, or to turn on the charm. Rick was perennially thin and dapper as James Bond, and could whip up a martini blindfolded while defending dipsomania to the newly initiated, and was capable of enduring the haughtiest clients and the most intolerable boors. He gave back what he got and they swallowed it hook, line, and sinker.

I tried to hook up with him once. I was trashed and suffering from a broken marriage and it seemed like a good idea at the time. Rick sent me home in a cab, alone and unhanded, and although I've tried not to think about it over the past years, I know he has. I pretend not to notice. We're close and we're friends, a difficult relationship to maintain in any business, especially one as transient as ours.

A young man in a grease-covered grey uniform was holding a small metal box with coloured wires protruding from it. He had snake tattoos winding around his lower arms and a miniature radio with the sound quality of a kazoo stuck permanently in his shirt pocket.

"Hi, Ms. Walker, nice to see you again," he said, turning the volume down.

Bill had slightly stooped shoulders, caused, no doubt, from climbing around tiny crawl spaces filled with dripping pipes and broken machinery all day long.

"Hi, Bill, good to see you, too," I replied. Then I looked at Rick. "It got awfully quiet in here when I came in. What were you two talking about?"

"We're talking about parts," Rick answered.

"Female parts?" I asked, trying to be one of the boys. It never worked.

"Ha, ha, ha, if only that were funny," Rick mocked. "Refrigerator parts."

"You know we can't afford any more repairs. The hood fan just got fixed. I'm not made of money." I could hear my voice rising. "What could possibly be broken now?"

Rick continued to lean back in the chair, gazed up at the ceiling and said dryly, "Things haven't been this bad since the Spanish Inquisition."

"How do you mean?" I asked cautiously. Rick had a knack for derailing my tantrums with cryptic statements that might lead me into a verbal trap.

"What's with the third degree, Liz? The old salad bar reach-in needs a new compressor." I relaxed. He wasn't baiting me.

"Again...?"

"That was over six years ago."

Rick made the decisions about equipment replacement and general repairs. He loved to tinker and considered himself to be an ace mechanic. The basement was full of broken chairs, torn patio umbrellas, burned-out motors, and a mountain of other odds and ends that he refused to throw out, but seldom fixed. Occasionally I forced him to hire outside help.

Bill was an expert on compressors. We had three double-door refrigerated reach-in units, two standing singles, and a deep freezer in the kitchen. A massive, room-size walk-in dominated one of the basement walls and a glass-fronted beer cooler stood behind the dining-room bar. Since each refrigerator had its own compressor, Bill was around a lot more than we liked.

Rick was looking sideways at me while Bill pretended to examine the box more closely by holding it up to one eye. I waited for someone to break the silence and realized that would have to be me.

"Sorry, guys, my nerves are shot. The cat caught a mouse in the dining room. The chef hasn't shown up for lunch yet and the place is packed."

"Who's cooking?" Rick demanded.

"Ceymore."

"Ceymore!" he cried. He lifted his feet off the desk, thumping his soft Gucci loafers on the ancient floorboards. "Lord of the dingalings? He thinks *el dente* is Spanish for 'dentist.' I better get down there before he sets the place on fire." The chair went into a lopsided swivel as he jumped to his feet. "Come on, Bill. Let's see if we can get that old compressor going again."

I smiled affectionately after them and turned to look out the office bay window. An enameled sign on the corner lamppost read, FASHION DISTRICT. One of the day-pass patients from a neighbouring mental institution was modelling pajamas at the crosswalk below. He seemed to be mingling nicely with the crowd.

I was worried about our new chef. Things had been running amazingly well in the kitchen since Daniel Chapin had joined the team. His food was fantastic and news of his talent was creating a media buzz all over town. The food channel, something I didn't watch because I was actually "living the dream," had approached me about doing a cooking show. Not that I would of course, but it's nice to be asked. Business had doubled and I was catching up on overdue bills. Now, without any of the typical warning signs — moodiness or the cutting of shifts — our star was two hours late and nowhere to be found. I should have known better to think it would last.

A chef knows that ample preparation is half the battle to flawless execution in the pit. A collective effort always, one person short in the kitchen puts the entire operation out of sync. The food takes longer to deliver, the plates are hastily presented, and the flavors are inferior. Owing to the large table we had booked for lunch today and without Daniel in attendance, my impulse to fire him quickly evaporated.

The chance of finding a good chef in a city where a new restaurant opens every day was as slim as finding a pearl in an oyster shell and can someone please explain to me how a stint as a pizza maker qualifies a response to an "experienced chefs only" advertisement? Just because you can make a five-topping pizza and maybe a calzone to boot does not authorize you to ask what the hours would be. No hours, okay. Plus, there's an awful lot of sexism going on out there. How often have I wanted to reach through the phone and pull a guy's tonsils out when, for the third time, I have to tell him that he *is* speaking to the boss?

I'd do anything to get Daniel back. I picked up the phone and dialled his number. No answer. I slammed it back down again. As soon as I got back from grocery shopping, I'd hunt him down if it killed me.

The telephone rang. *Please, please*, I prayed, *let it be Daniel*.

"Haven't you left yet?" Rick demanded. "The meat order still hasn't come in. You better pick it up in the market while you're there and get three more lemongrass."

Rick liked bossing me around. I suggested he buy me out and I work for him, then he could yell at me with impunity. His response was if he wanted to lose a lot of money he'd go to Las Vegas. Despite his cavalier attitude, he was doing his best to prep the kitchen for lunch and I had to help.

I shopped for produce, bakery, and specialty items on a day-to-day basis while the large orders consisting of dairy, fish, and meat were delivered by truck to the restaurant two or three times a week. It was getting late and since the meat order hadn't arrived, I'd better hurry.

I grabbed some cash from the safe sitting in a corner of the office. Small as a breadbox and heavy as lead, the fifty-year-old safe was formerly housed in the restaurant, but thieves kept stealing it and abandoning it in the alleyway. The staff would find it and haul it back in along with a few additional dents to the thick armored sides. Not much cash in the safe these days, mostly credit card vouchers or debit receipts, and definitely no diamonds in little black bags.

For a king's ransom, Rick and I were allowed "in and out" privileges in the busy car park across the street. I passed Rick's luxury minivan with its shiny, waxed exterior and pristine interior, and, looking through the window of my rusty old sedan with inches of festering clutter on the floor, knew a stomach-turning unidentifiable odour from the back seat would be waiting for me when I slid inside. Rick refused to ride in my car without a wetsuit, saying that he was too afraid something would attach itself to his leg. Seriously, I told him, try lugging around raw meat and fish every day and see what his car smelled like.

Kensington Market, one of the oldest and most diverse shopping areas in Toronto, was situated between two major thoroughfares: Spadina Avenue and Bathurst Street. The criss-crossing mesh of narrow streets could confuse the most seasoned traveller. Hundreds of storefronts, converted from traditional family homes into individual market spaces, competed with one another for the few straggling shoppers to buy their goods.

Worn down and neglected, the market was coming to ruin. No wrought-iron benches on which to stop or rest a heavy bag, and forget about festive Christmas lights in December or flower baskets hanging from streetlamps in the summer. Instead, the word "pussy" had been scribbled across several of the boarded storefronts. One empty building lot had become repository for stained mattresses and rotting garbage. Not enough parking for busy days; except there haven't been any in a long time and many of the old store owners were growing weary waiting for the city to remember and the crowds to return.

Personally, I wouldn't shop anywhere else. I like to see what I'm buying. The produce was always fresh and handpicked by me. Rather than be delivered by large commercial trucks and dropped off at the back door — a case of rotting lettuce could screw up the entire day. There was nothing quite as prickly as a chef with bad greens on his hands. Plus, the cheese was mercifully affordable and not wrapped in sheets of plastic, which is akin to cheese homicide and should be punishable by death.

Buckets of homegrown flowers and containers of fruit and vegetables sat outdoors under brightly coloured awnings. Music piped out to the street allowed shoppers to stride along in gaited rhythm while roasted coffee and heady incense mingled in the air with the faintest hint of urine just to keep you on your toes.

Traffic was gridlocked on Spadina Avenue. Cars were making U-turns, bouncing dangerously over the streetcar tracks in an attempt to avoid the congestion up ahead. I swerved right, fishtailing through an oily puddle onto a short service lane marked NO EXIT, and, ignoring the warning, drove along a series of narrow alleyways leading me into the heart of Chinatown and eventually out above the traffic jam. The street I needed to turn on to was blocked by a black police cruiser with rotating blue-and-red lights.

Eddie, short for Eduardo, was waving furiously at me from the street corner.

Normally Eddie would save me a space in front of his grandfather's fruit store where he and his family, the Contraros, have lived, in the same overhead apartment, for three generations. He flagged me over, yelling at the top of his lungs, "Lizzie, Lizzie!"

Eddie's the only person who can call me Lizzie without suffering the dire consequences. Rick said he'd rather nail his testicles to the floor than live through the horror again.

"What's going on, Eddie?" I asked, poking my head out the car window.

"Big accident, big accident," he shouted some more. He was really excited and between outbursts of giggles, he told me repeatedly that the street was closed — gee, thanks, Eddie I can see that — but that I could park in his grandfather's spot behind the store.

Eddie was somewhere in the age group between eleven and thirty-two. His mind wasn't going to grow any older than a child's, although his body was beginning to show its years. Tiny lines had formed around his dark eyes and a small paunch had grown noticeable. He wore a red nylon jacket done up to his chin, grey sweat pants, and high-top basketball runners with the tongues sticking out. Granted, he may not have been dealt a full hand, but he played his cards cheerfully. I pulled down the cramped alley, leaving my car wedged in between a row of empty wooden apple crates. Emerging from the laneway onto Augusta Street, I was stopped by a young policeman.

"Sorry, miss, you'll have to return to your car. The market is temporarily off limits."

"I'm picking up my meat order from Superior Meats," I chirped.

Feet planted firmly apart, hands on hips, he announced, "It's closed for today."

"That's ridiculous! It's Friday, they're always open Friday."

"They're closed."

I leaned around the cop to see what was happening. Except for a few curious shopkeepers, the street was deserted. Yellow caution tape was strung across the road in front of the meat shop. Newspaper covered the store's large expansive windows and a fleet of squad cars lined the street. Two black, unmarked vans were parked near Superior's front door with their rear doors wide open.

Across the street, I noticed that the owner of the Cheese Emporium was watching me and I waved to her.

"Hi, Louise!" I hollered.

"Hey, Blondie!" she hollered back.

"Have you got my order ready to pick up?"

She hesitated for a heartbeat, looked at the cop barring my way, and replied, "It's been ready for an hour, come and get it before I unpack it."

I smiled sweetly at the young cop, flirtatiously mouthing the word "please?"

"Hurry up," he warned, apparently inured to my wily ways. "I'm not supposed to let anyone in." Before he had second thoughts, I charged across the street and through the screen door Louise Kozinski was holding open for me.

Once again, I was brought up short by the sight of towering columns of cheese leaning heavily against one another for support. There were so many varieties it was impossible to remember all the names. A handwritten sign taped to a swizzle stick announced her latest tasty treat was "Drunken Goat Cheese Cheddar." An end piece had already been cut off the block of cheese, revealing a purple-and-gold checkerboard pattern inside. I took some home for a poker game last week, but the food wimps took a pass.

"Pass the chips, please."

Shelves running the entire length of the store were loaded with biscotti, shortbread, and sugary wafers. The back wall of the store was stacked from end to end with pasta noodles in every conceivable shape, their bright cellophane wrappers crackling testily when handled. Giant pickles wadded into jars, imported from Hungary and other pickle Meccas from around the world, crowded around the register. Layers of smoked meats and fish, which set off a quivering hunger in me, filled the deep, glass-topped refrigerated chest. I gazed lovingly around the store, deciding I could live there quite comfortably for a very long time.

Louise startled me out of my reverie. "So what about that order?" she demanded.

"So, what's going on?" I snapped back.

"You haven't been in for three weeks and now you want information? Well, it will cost, my friend," she said, grinning.

Louise knows my name, but I either get called Blondie or "my friend." Frankly, I prefer Blondie, because everybody who comes in that door is called "my friend" and I figured out a long time ago that it's her secret code word for asshole.

Hello, my friend. What can I get for you, my friend? Would you like another free sample, my friend? You get the picture.

After taking my order, Louise strolled to the back of the store and opened the door to the enameled reach-in. She lugged out a hefty block of white cheddar and dropped it onto an enormous wood block. Until now, I hadn't realized how hefty she was becoming herself. Wearing a wine-coloured wraparound dress made of clingy jersey and elasticized around the middle, she looked like a two-hundred-pound blood sausage. The neckline of the dress was gaping at the crossover, revealing a cotton white slip like the kind my grandmother used to wear.

Smoothly, as if it were soft ice cream, she sliced a kilo from the chunk of hard cheese and started to wrap it in brown waxed paper. The door opened behind me, jangling the bells hung from its frame. Louise launched into her routine.

"Hello my friend … oh!" she abruptly went silent.

I turned to see a badge held out for us to read; a big man with a wide chest, not heavy or fat, but solid as a brick wall, stood in the doorway behind me.

"Sorry to interrupt you, ladies. I am Detective Winn. If you don't mind answering a few questions, I won't be long."

I tried to brush past him as if he weren't speaking to me, too, but he stepped directly in front of me, blocking my exit.

"Could I get your name, too, please, ma'am?" he asked.

Ma'am? When did I go from being a miss to a ma'am? Besides, judging by his mildly receding hairline, this guy looked about the same age as me, although something told me he was in way better shape. I'm thin, well, mostly. Lately I've been starting to spread out in various directions. Nevertheless, I gave it the old college try for him. I sucked in my stomach and fluffed my hair. The policeman stared down at his notepad, smirking slightly to himself and suddenly I felt ancient. Some days I looked much younger than my years, others, not so much. Maybe it was the earrings. I never liked these earrings, too big, like miniature crystal balls. I was throwing them out the second I got home. He coughed and I realized he was staring at me.

"My name is Elizabeth Walker, Mr. Winn," I announced crisply.

The day was warming, causing him to remove his jacket. He slung it casually over one shoulder and rolled up the sleeves of his powder-blue shirt, leaving tan, muscular arms exposed. I was compelled to touch his forearm, but sensibly refrained.

"That's Detective Winn, Ms. Walker. My officer posted at the alleyway entrance tells me that you're picking up an order."

He stopped, waiting for me to jump in with details. I didn't, but I did have the urge to touch his arm again.

He asked, "Do you live in the area, Ms. Walker?"

"It's Liz, and no, I have a restaurant close by though. It's called Walker's Way."

The smile faded and his eyes went dark.

"Just a few blocks away from here," I added. "South of Chinatown,"

"I know where it is," the stern-faced policeman said flatly. "My wife and I had our last meal there. She told me she was leaving me after the first course. We didn't get to the second."

I winced. First dates, proposals, fiftieth-anniversary celebrations, and breakup dates. I've seen it all. I wanted to tell him that it could have been worse.

A woman followed her husband to the restaurant one evening and confronted him at his table. She screamed at the lying bastard (her words not mine) for ten minutes while his mistress slunk away and hid in the washroom. The customers, utterly fascinated by the free side show and motivated by the "better him than me" philosophy, continued to drink. Liquor sales soared that night.

Somehow, I didn't think this little anecdote would make him feel any better and kept quiet.

"I understand you buy your meat supplies from Superior Meats. Is that why you're here today?" the detective inquired.

"Yes, our meat order didn't show up this morning. We pick up other supplies on a daily basis so I thought I'd get it while I was here."

"Does that happen often?"

"What?"

"Your order doesn't get delivered?"

"It happens. A truck breaks down, the order is misplaced or isn't large enough for delivery. And sometimes the chef merely forgets to call it in after a long night."

"Your chef's name is?" His pen was poised in mid-air.

"Daniel Chapin."

"How do you spell that?"

"Like the composer only with an *a*." I started to spell it for him. "C-H-A ..."

The detective cut me off. "Thanks. I got the rest of it. Is he at the restaurant now?"

"No. He didn't come into work today." I wanted to vent, but now probably wasn't a good time.

"According to Superior Meats' office answering machine, someone from your restaurant called last night around midnight. We traced the number. The message was cut off. Do you think he was putting an order in?"

"Probably, although it sounds a bit late, I guess it varies from night to night. I'm not usually there at that time."

"You must have some idea."

"Okay, I'd say any time after nine o'clock, after the dinner rush was over. He'd know what we needed for the next day by then."

"And do you know what time he finished work last night?"

"Not at the moment, but I can look it up on the signout sheet."

"Thank you, Ms. Walker, just one more question. Were you familiar with Mr. Anthony Vieira, the owner of Superior Meats?"

"Call me Liz, and how do you mean *familiar?*"

"How well did you know him?"

"I know his employees called him Mr. Tony and I avoided him when I was in the store. He gave me the creeps."

"That seems to be an opinion expressed by others," he said. "However, what I meant was did you have more than a business relationship with him?"

"Perhaps, Detective, you should say what you mean and certainly not." I got the feeling he was being purposely obtuse.

"That's all for now, Ms. Walker, but I would like to ask you a few more questions. I can meet you at your restaurant later this afternoon if that's all right. Would that be convenient?"

I was fairly convinced it didn't matter if it was or not. "Fine by me, but I don't even know what's happened yet."

"A body was found early this morning by one of Superior Meats' employees. We assume it's the owner of the store, Anthony Vieira."

"What do you mean, *assume?*"

"We can't be sure it's him until we get a positive DNA identification. The body was unrecognizable."

I wasn't sure I wanted to know the answer, but I couldn't help ask the question. "How unrecognizable?"

"He was butchered and his body parts wrapped up in parcels with the initials W.W. on them. Those would be same as your restaurant's, wouldn't they?"

chapter two

I was dying to tell Rick the news, but when I called him from the market he was too busy to talk. Detective Winn had deliberately tried to shock me with the gory news of Mr. Tony's demise, and then, seeing that I might faint, asked Louise to get me a glass of water. She dragged a stool from behind the counter for me to sit on and hovered over my shoulder. The detective apologized for his bluntness and reminded me he would come to the restaurant later that day for an "ah, more private," interview. Louise huffed at the suggestion she was being nosy, and, crossing her arms in front of her, didn't budge. The policeman shook his head tiredly and left.

By the time I returned to Walker's, I was spilling over with excitement. Unfortunately, Daniel still hadn't appeared for his shift, making last-minute changes to the menu a priority. Rick left a message for our sous-chef, Michael, to come in as soon as he returned from Montreal visiting "his parents," a well-known euphemism for "drunken orgy."

Rick knew the menu; he just didn't like to cook. The more complicated menu items would have to be nixed. There was only so much my manager, an inexperienced line man, and a dishwasher were qualified to do. The waiters would write up a replacement menu offering the dishes we were capable of serving, thus preventing a routine similar to a Monty Python sketch: *Do you have any steak? Yes, but not today.*

I had picked up three boxes of vegetables, a kilo of cheese, two bags of white, a bag of bones, and half a dozen Supremes from the market's main poultry store. Since Superior Meats was closed, I was unable to get our meat order, and, to put it mildly, Rick would not be pleased. I did remember to pick up a ten-pound sack of wood-chip flour, which we needed to burn in our homemade smoker.

Because I was saving all my money to buy a replacement arm for the upright Hobart mixer, it left no room in the budget to purchase a new smoker box. Instead, the chef was required to fabricate a facsimile and each had his own method. Daniel was good at it. He molded a thick sheet of industrial aluminum foil into a two-foot-tall teepee, complete with a chimney and a miniature fire pit. He sprinkled the ground wood chips on the bottom and then lit it.

In order to obtain the smokiest flavor in the salmon and turkey pieces, the correct consistency of sawdust is crucial for burning. If the grains are too fine, the fire won't catch, and if the grains are too large, you'll start a raging bonfire — something to keep in mind when doing this indoors. I learned this the hard way.

In my defense, using the chef's hat to smother the flames seemed like a good idea at the time and I don't know why I'm not allowed to start the fire anymore. Anyway, after a few hours in the smoldering, smoke-filled teepee, the meats are tender and tasty, ready to be served on our very popular open-faced sandwiches.

In less than an hour, twenty hungry architects would be rolling through Walker's front door, looking for lunch. In an attempt to drum up business, I had dropped off a menu to their new offices situated in a converted furrier warehouse less than a half block away. It worked like a charm and their firm was trying us out for the first time today. Unfortunately, the way things were going, it would likely be their last. If diners come in two or three times before you drop the ball, they tend to chalk it up as human error. We needed to build a winning rapport with the architects before I could expect them to be so forgiving.

When I pulled the car up to the back of the restaurant, the kitchen boys burst through the delivery door descending on the supplies like a gang of scavengers. The car's trunk was popped, its doors yanked open, and anything resembling food was whisked away.

Rick was really keyed up and immediately tore into me. "What took so long? Did you go out for dim sum while you were there?"

I liked it better when the chef was in the kitchen. I wouldn't have to race around town picking up last-minute supplies and I wouldn't have to face Rick afterwards. I appreciated his pitching in to save the day, but by the time lunch is over, his sarcasm will have reached a scathing dryness capable of reducing even the most cynical to tears. I've had to rescue many a cowering waiter over the years, not to mention the demoralized prep cook, Ceymore.

Being short-staffed like this, he knew all too well what to expect. I ignored his attitude.

"You wouldn't believe it, Rick, there was a murder in the market. The whole place was cordoned off by the police."

"Just my luck. What happened?"

"I'm not sure about the details. They think it was Anthony Vieira, the owner of Superior Meats."

"Good. I didn't like him, anyway. The guy was a pig." He turned around and I followed him inside.

"That's not a nice thing to say," I told him.

"I'm not nice."

"You are to me."

"Easily rectified ..."

"Seriously ..."

Rick picked up the bag of sawdust, transferring it to a stainless-steel table shelf, where a sheet of foil waited.

"Everybody knew what a dick he was," he said, turning around. "He bragged about how beautiful his wife was and then hit on everything that moved. I believe he hit on you, too, didn't he?"

"Yeah, once, a hundred years ago maybe, but for heaven's sake, the police think ..."

I realized Rick had stopped listening to me the second he stuck his head in the oven and screamed that the pilot light had gone out again. I made a timely departure, zipping past the mayhem in the kitchen through the swinging door that led into the dining room.

It was love at first sight when I purchased this old diner and it still was. After decades of hard service followed by neglect and abuse — the last owners used it for a late-night craps joint — the place needed a lot of tender loving care to return it to its former glory.

Garish neon lights suspended from bushy frayed cords attached to the ceiling were replaced with the milky glass globes I found buried under forty years of powdery insect dust in the basement. The striated oak-veneered booths were painstakingly stripped by hand and varnished. The walls were patched and painted a rich cream colour. Nothing contrived or carbon copied here, just a lot of elbow grease and wishful thinking. The ceilings were fifteen feet high like they were in the rest of the three-storied building and were covered in pressed tin that would cost a fortune to reproduce today.

The front room was long and narrow. The booths ran down the entire length on one side and a tongue-and groove-counter ran halfway along the other. The countertop was a pockmarked, heavily veined marble whose porous surface had permanently stained over the years. It resembled the same shade of dappled weak tea captured in a fading sepia photograph I discovered in the crowded files of the Historical Board Archives. It was dated 1905 and looked virtually the same.

A row of stools running the length of the bar had been screwed to the floor sometime in the fifties and except for a thousand pieces of old gum stuck to the underside of the chrome tops, they looked genuinely the same. The vinyl clad seats rotated on iron spindles, which, unfortunately because of their age, caused the metal to squeak. While their parents sipped wine, the kids spun the seats around and around until the squealing made my ears bleed.

A pot flew past the kitchen door window. I tried reaching Daniel by phone again, but all I got was his answering machine. I had to find him before the police did, drag him back to Walker's, and persuade him to work. Rick would last a day at the most. There was just enough time before lunch to take a drive out to the city's east end and pay our missing chef a visit. I knew where he lived. A few months ago I had given him a lift home after work when his car was in the shop. I was surprised to discover that he lived fairly close to my house and even more surprised at his suggestion I come inside to unwind. Although extremely tempted, I said no.

It's not that he wasn't attractive. His face had finely chiselled features and dark, thick brows with sultry eyes that languished underneath long lashes. He was barely taller than my five foot nine, but his body was lean and gangly, a natural bad-boy type who had to beat women off with a stick. Proof of why I find it unfathomable that the image of a chef conjures up the fat, jolly, Chef Boyardee stereotype.

Unfortunately, it's also been my experience that most chefs should be institutionalized. They're either insane because of their dependency on addictive stress relievers or intolerable because they don't use any. I claim it's the heat, the smoke, and the barely controlled chaos. The limited time frame to be creative, the pressure for every dish to be perfect, and if not, the shame! It had been a while since my last relationship with a cook, more like a decade, but I knew better than to get involved with Daniel. When the time came for him to disappear, like now for example, I'd end up getting hurt and it wouldn't be the first time.

Daniel lived on the south side of Queen Street East, and I lived on the north. Our neighbourhoods were close to a picturesque residential community situated on the shores of Lake Ontario aptly named the Beaches. With a mile-long boardwalk and high real-estate prices to match, I couldn't afford to buy a house there now.

When I first moved into my neighbourhood, it was dominated by blue-collar workers content with tidy green lawns and plastic ornaments and who were blissfully unaware of current design trends. Several years later, the area was "discovered" and every other house was gutted and reassembled in the best of tastes. Not my house. I bought it after my marriage broke up and have been slowly painting over the yellowing walls ever since. No time for renovation or the inclination, I'm afraid. I got my fill of that at the restaurant.

Daniel lived in a townhouse with a cinder-block garage situated directly under the house. Connecting it to the road was a dangerously steep driveway. It was obvious why his block was being overlooked by the real-estate speculators. On the corner of the street, a service station was stockpiling tires in an enclosed side yard patrolled by a slobbering German Shepherd. As I drew near, the dog leaped onto the chain-link fence, hooked his claws through the metal links, and hung halfway from the top — a clever manoeuvre that allowed it to bark ferociously and simultaneously expose himself as I drove by.

Attached to Daniel's boxy townhouse were four identical others with similar wrought-iron verandahs and corrugated-plastic overhangs. The two remaining original grand homes on the other side of the street were hidden behind overgrown bushes and covered with long, ropy vines, suitable perhaps for ghouls or grow-ops, but not much more.

When I found Daniel's place, I was surprised to see the garage door up and his car parked inside. I walked up the five cement steps and knocked. No answer. I waited a minute and then put my ear up to the door. The house was quiet. Maybe Daniel was sleeping. I knocked harder. Maybe he was sick. I used my fists. Nothing. Giving up on the front door, I walked down the steps into the garage, hoping to find another door to the house.

I had to squeeze around his vehicle, which took up most of the allowable space, when the smell hit me like a brick. You don't need to own a restaurant to recognize the high stench of rotting meat and my nose told me it was coming from Daniel's trunk. I tried to lift it but it wouldn't budge. Spotting a rusty crowbar leaning in a corner, I bent over to pick it up.

"Don't touch that!" Detective Winn yelled, making me jump. I dropped the crowbar, sending it clanking to the ground.

"What are you doing here?" I yelled back in shock.

"That's precisely what I'd like to ask you, Ms. Walker."

I replied more calmly than I felt. "Call me Liz, and I'm trying to find my chef. This is Daniel's car and whatever's in that trunk smells pretty bad. I think we should take a look."

Winn stepped between me and the back of Daniel's car. "I'll take it from here, thank you, Ms. Walker and then, if you don't mind, I'd like to talk to you in private." He issued a command to one of the officers, "Sergeant, escort Ms. Walker to the cruiser and have her wait in the car."

I gave up telling the detective to call me Liz. All business and no play, this one.

He pointed at another young man. "Constable, put your gloves on. Let's get this trunk open."

The sergeant and I walked quietly side by side to the curb. I was about to climb in the back seat when another cruiser pulled alongside. The driver waved at the officer, who briefly let go of my arm in order to wave back. I tore out of his grasp and ran back down the driveway, hopping sideways between the car and garage wall. Holding my nose, I looked directly into the trunk.

Six cases of New York sirloins, stinking to high heaven, were marked:

DELIVERY — C.N.E.

Winn slammed the trunk shut, and propelled me by my elbow back to my car.

"I told you this morning I would meet you at the restaurant. What are you doing here? " His softly rugged facial features had transformed into a harsh, uninviting landscape. He was trying to keep his voice down.

"You better check the house to see if Daniel's in there." I said, craning my neck around his wide shoulder. "He could be hurt."

"I want you out of here, now!"

"I thought you wanted to talk to me."

"Now! Do you understand?" He was yelling again.

I slammed my car door in his face and laid rubber on the pavement. Time to make a hasty retreat, or at least pretend to. I wasn't leaving yet. I drove around the block to Eastern Avenue.

The surrounding area was a mixture of new residential and commercial enterprises taking over defunct industrial warehouses. Film studios had replaced many of the empty factories. I had a look at one of the new condominium lofts and thought the mortgage payments were reasonable until the realtor pointed out that was the monthly maintenance fee.

I parked the car at the end of Daniel's street behind a stage mobile unit with orange cones marked "film" placed around it. I had a clear view of Winn on the phone. I picked up a cone, put it beside my car, and continued to watch. A few minutes later an unmarked van pulled into Daniel's driveway. Two men in white dust suits emerged, nodded at Winn, and went down into the garage, carrying large, green, plastic tote containers. They returned, I assumed, with the load of putrid steaks packed inside. Depositing them into the back of the van, they gave Winn a paper to sign and left.

By now I thought someone from the trailer would come out and retrieve the cone. But nobody was around, probably at lunch. LUNCH! I quickly called the restaurant. One of my favorite waiters picked up the phone.

"Walker's Way, Marshall here, how may I be of service?" His singsong voice held just the right amount of ingratiating professionalism.

"Marshall, it's Liz, I need to talk to Rick. How's he doing?"

"As well as can be expected under the circumstances, I'll get him for you."

The phone was put down on the marble bar top, which clearly transmitted the sounds coming from the kitchen. I could hear Rick in the background, vitriolic comments pouring out of his mouth.

"WHAT?" he roared into the mouthpiece.

"Rick, I'm at Daniel's place and the cops are here. You wouldn't believe what I found in the trunk of his car."

"You better tell me you found chef in it because if he isn't dead I'm going to kill him myself. I've got a table of miserable fucking architects who don't feel like eating chicken today, three burned cheesecakes, and a pot full of soggy pasta, thanks to Ceymore, the great incompetent."

Rick doesn't use birth names for our chefs, just "Chef." After ten years he gave up trying to remember their names. Only a few are ever memorable. Those are the ones we pay homage to, dance around, lick their boots. I actually thought Rick liked Daniel. I heard him use his real name once.

"Listen, I don't know what's going on, but it definitely involves Daniel. The cops are breaking into his house now. I'm hiding in my car, watching them."

"So you're in your car relaxing and I'm up to my eyeballs in orders I can't fill."

"I'm not relaxing. I'm on a stakeout."

"Please tell me you didn't just say the word 'stakeout.'"

"Rick, something weird is happening, I've got to go." I could hear Rick telling me not to hang up while I did precisely that.

The police broke into Daniel's house. After a few minutes, they came stomping back out. Winn snapped a few orders to the policemen, then took off in his unmarked sedan. The house must have been empty inside. Everyone left except for one cop to stand guard.

The truth was, I half-expected to discover Daniel's body in his car trunk. After what happened at Superior Meats, I thought there might be a serial killer on the loose. I certainly didn't expect to see a thousand dollars' worth of rotting steak in his trunk, which I knew didn't belong to me. I never buy more meat than I can sell in three days because pawning off beef stew as the daily special for a week gets mighty boring, not to mention a little dicey.

I decided to leave, but I didn't want to head back to the restaurant just yet. Rick would make me feel guilty and I'd wind up doing the dishes or washing lettuce, an equally hideous job. The lunch rush would be over by the time I returned, so why poke my head in a hornet's nest? I drove along Eastern Avenue for a few minutes, went south down Carlaw Avenue, and turned right on to Lake Shore Drive.

During the horse-and-buggy days, the "Lake Shore" route may have been considered a scenic drive around Lake Ontario and still could be, except that the marshlands were filled over sixty years ago to accommodate industrial plants, warehouses, and garbage depots that have remained, changed, and multiplied over the decades. A story that my eighty-year-old neighbour, Mr. Mullen, shared with me years ago haunts me every time I drive past the spot on my way downtown.

Mr. Mullen was born in the house across the street from mine in 1925. His story relies on his memory, which appears to be sharp as a tack. The trains still continue to speed by daily on the railroad tracks that lay behind his now fenced-in backyard. In his youth, there was a brick quarry on the other side of those tracks where he and the other children used to swim, until there was a terrible tragedy. A child drowned in the deep, muddy waters. The quarry was drained and pronounced unsafe and shortly afterwards it was commissioned for use as a city garbage dump. To make way for the new subway garage that fills the acre pit site today, the garbage was hauled out years later and buried underground. Undisturbed landfill slowly decomposes under lakeside fields covered with mature maple trees and flocks of Canadian geese. Contained by barbed-wire fencing, the grassy mounds appear to be abundantly fertile, ditto the geese.

I continued driving west on Lakeshore Drive past unused acreage that remains between the road and the canal front that joins the Don River. A burgeoning homeless resort made up of tarps and tents that squatted on the empty land was eventually bulldozed. The irony that the property belonged to a mega department store, selling do- it-yourself home-improvement materials, wasn't wasted on the good people of Toronto.

Ducking under the Gardiner Expressway overpass, I ignored the small armies of isolated men working to repair the struts and spans that allowed run off rainwater to shower the cars below. Aiming directly for one of these waterfalls, I slowed down and got a mini car wash. It wasn't clean water, but a shower is a shower and adequate enough to remove the anonymously scribbled messages from the car's rear window. "SUCK ME" was the latest in a series of rude suggestions. Others are too foul to repeat aloud.

As I rounded the lake, a tip of a wing appeared first, then the rest of her majestic figure loomed into sight. High atop a colossal arch, an angel fanned alabaster wings across two wrought-iron sentry gates flanking both sides of her perch. The theme song "Let's all go to the Ex" cued automatically in my mind.

The "Ex" or "C.N.E.," short for Canadian National Exhibition, opened in 1880. When the summer fair is on during the last three weeks of August, you can't get near the place. You have to park two miles away and walk in the blistering heat to the gate entrance. I remembered begging my parents to carry me, crying shamelessly until they did.

The ticket booths surrounding the entrance to the grounds had been removed, the massive gates opened wide to allow traffic through. I looked up at the angel as I drove under her wings. Still a thrill!

Cars parked bumper to bumper along the empty midway filled the massive void left by carnival rides and game booths. Except for white lines painted like hopscotch patterns fading on the tarmac, it was hard to believe that less than a month ago the grounds were swarming with thousands of visitors.

A steady stream of trucks and vans passed me on both sides of the main avenue of the grounds. Following the line of traffic to the convention centre, I passed a newly erected grey box of a building contrasting starkly with its historic neighbour, the impressive horse pavilion. A noticeable group of cable television trucks and a news van were on the sidewalk. More noticeably, two police cars and one unmarked beige cruiser idled beside them. I slowed down and recognized Detective Winn climbing the front steps of the hall. I parked in an illegal space that miraculously opened up, and then I joined a small crowd filing determinedly through a side door near the rear of the building. I didn't want to bump into the detective if I could help it.

I stepped behind the others into a small, utilitarian lobby from which several hallways sprouted in different directions. No one was lingering. Most likely they were responding to a call for an important staff meeting. I hesitated, trying to decide which group to follow, when a voice in the fast-moving crowd behind me sounded familiar.

"Liz Walker, are you taking tables tonight?" I turned, recognizing Martin Wright, a former waiter of mine, and jostling shoulders affectionately, we walked together, keeping pace with the others.

"Marty, how are you?" I exclaimed. "How's the band? I saw you in that beer commercial," I rattled on while taking in his new look. "You were fabulous, dahhling."

Martin had let his hair, once a closely shorn crew cut, grow out into a mass of blond curls, which I actually thought suited him better, and, without wanting to stare, picked up on a hint of eyeliner.

"Thanks, Liz, we made a few bucks, but the band broke up. We argued all the time. Stardom didn't suit us, I guess. That's why I'm here, I'm pulling a double. I need the money. What are you doing here?"

"I'm trying to find someone," I answered truthfully. "I know you usually work the big winter fair in November, but I didn't know there was a show in April, too."

"This is strictly a cattle show, kind of a prelim to the winter fair. First one, very United Nations, you know."

"Is that being held here? I thought it would be somewhere ritzy like the Sutton Place."

"Not if you want to bring your prize bulls with you, baby. Hey, one of your chefs is working the show."

I knew it. Daniel was moonlighting and standing me up at the same time. I could feel my temper rising and realized Martin was asking me something.

"He's adorable. Is he single?"

"No, Martin. He's AWOL."

"Sorry, Liz. What happened?"

"He didn't show up for work and Rick is covering for him."

"Uh-oh, that can't be good. Glad I'm not working there anymore."

"I know, he's in a terrible mood. I need to talk to Daniel. Where's the kitchen?"

"They won't let you in without a pass. A couple of guests got food poisoning."

Those are words people in my business never want to hear. I gasped. "You're kidding?"

"No, I'm not, and it's hush-hush. Nobody wants the press to make a big deal out of it. Bad image for the first day of the show."

"Are they going to be okay?" I asked.

"Who knows? Two people were rushed to the hospital after the eating a breakfast of steak and eggs."

"When did that happen?"

"This morning at a private press-release ceremony," replied Martin.

There seemed to be an awful lot of bad meat floating around these days, which reminded me why I was there. I had trouble believing that Daniel would be stupid enough to blow us off for another gig. Sooner or later, a chef's reputation catches up with them. And Daniel was no exception. A phone call to one of the restaurants listed on his resumé hinted he was trouble, but the owner revealed nothing. The man refused to discuss Daniel's history in detail. I wasn't concerned. Most follow-up references were a waste of time. Recommending a lousy chef to another restaurant was a dirty joke to play on your competition, but it's happened to me more times than I care to remember.

A year ago after a brief telephone conversation with a highly respected chef of a chic uptown hot spot, and entirely on his say-so, I hired a previous cook of his who had listed him as a reference. I knew we were in trouble when on his first day our new chef was visited by three burly thugs with deep foreign accents. As a precautionary rule, no one is allowed in the kitchen during service except staff, so you can imagine my surprise when one of the waiters complained that the kitchen door was blocked on the inside by a customer.

I managed to squeeze through the door, demanding with great authority that they leave at once. One of the men, who was licking his fingers and looking at me as if he would like to use me for a toothpick, said, "Nice place you got here, lady." I bought them a round of vodka shooters and they left without incident. Not surprisingly, the new chef didn't come in the next day.

The labour board doesn't allow character assass-ination that would purposely damage an employee's chances for a job elsewhere. Admittedly, Daniel's former employer said he could cook, which was all Rick wanted to hear. You know the saying, "Too many chefs, not enough cooks." Rick liked to say, "Too many chefs and none can cook." We were so hungry for talent that we didn't care if Daniel was an axe murderer. A conceit I was starting to regret.

Over the years, a few of our former chefs made it to the big time, but via the restaurant grapevine, we were often saddened to hear many had lost the battle to booze and pills, divorce, or anonymity.

Until now, Daniel hadn't caused us any problems, making me suspect it was merely a case of sour grapes between him and his former employer.

"Listen, Liz, I have to run," Martin said. "I'll drop into the restaurant soon and have a drink with you."

This last part was added as he quickened his pace down a service hall. He opened a door for the men's change room and whispered, "The kitchen is up ahead. Keep going and follow your nose." He blew me a kiss over his shoulder and disappeared inside.

I already felt better. At least I'd have my one-on-one with Daniel and ask for an explanation. I was ready to forgive him and offer him more money if that's what it took to get him back. On second thought, I didn't want to get ahead of myself. I'd try begging on my hands and knees first.

Similar to the Rogers Centre, the myriad doors, tunnels, and ramps making up the hall were a labyrinth of confusion. I never go to the washroom during a baseball game. I missed a whole inning once trying to find my way back to my seat. I thought I was lost when a door opened beyond me and I heard the distinct *whoosh*ing sound of a commercial dishwasher. This was likely an exterior work area where the dishes would be circulated and garbage hauled up those long ramps out to the recycling bins.

I got a whiff of grilled red peppers with a hint of rosemary thrown in, or someone was smoking marijuana:

the two odours smell remarkably the same to me. The kitchens were definitely here. The door locked shut before I could get to it, but I was confident there would be more doors up ahead. I hoped Daniel was behind one of them. Rounding the bend in the hall, I bumped into a gigantic security guard. He wore a black uniform and a high-tech head set.

"Sorry, miss, this area is closed."

"Hi, I own Walker's Way Bistro and was hoping to have a few words with my chef. He's helping with the event and I'd like to speak to him for a second."

"What's his name?"

"Daniel Chapin."

His eyes grew wary. He spoke into a black-tipped metal tube, the thickness of a pencil, which ran from his mouth to his ear and consulted a list of names on a clipboard. His hand was pressed to his ear, obviously listening to a response from the other end. I thought he was stalling, but when he looked up, he seemed relieved.

"Chapin doesn't work here anymore." Seeing my surprise, he added, "He quit, I guess." Having exhausted his quota of chit-chat for the moment, or perhaps the decade, the guard spun his massive bulk around as daintily as a ballerina and swiftly retreated into the nether regions from which he appeared.

My stomach rumbled and I realized with all the driving around searching for Daniel, I had missed lunch. I was hungry and longing for a glass of our newly listed Zinfandel wine. Imagining the velvety rope of ruby-red liquid wrapping sumptuously round my tongue, I smacked my lips and thought about heading back to Walker's for lunch. I've been eating in my own restaurant for over a decade and can't say I'm bored with the concept yet. I can order anything I want from the menu and if I don't see anything I like, I ask the chef to make me something special. Then I remembered Rick was cooking today and decided a glass of wine and a salad from the cold kitchen would suffice.

I got lost down another corridor and was about to retrace my steps when I heard a phone ringing. Another door swung open and I heard talking.

"I am not going to be held responsible. This was your grand scheme and I will not be part of it."

The voice was hoarse, strained, and loud. It sounded like Daniel, but I couldn't be sure.

I raced toward the voice. Suddenly, the hallway was filled with light from three overhead spots, and, not wanting to be caught snooping, I bent over a water fountain attached to the wall, pretending to get a drink. Like a fawn, I innocently sipped at the bubbling water until a blow of searing pain shot straight through the back of my head and raced to my knees. For one brief second I watched a candy cane of blood swirl around the white enamel basin and down the drain until my hand slipped off the handle.

When I woke up, I was sitting in a dentist chair with the grim Winn at my side. My head felt heavy and my mouth was all twisted. I tried speaking, but a nurse stuck a suction tube on my tongue to collect a bucket of drool. Winn saw my eyes open and came to my side. The doctor removed the bib and helped me sit up.

"Well, Mrs. Walker, the light sedation I gave you while I examined your wound is wearing off. You're at St. Michael's Hospital. Do you know where that is?"

I nodded my head — big mistake.

"The X-rays show no skull fractures, just bruising in this area here."

He went to touch it and I cringed in my chair. Detective Winn rolled his eyes.

"I can't do much about the chip in your front tooth right now," the doctor said. "The force of the hit to the back of your head jammed your mouth into the faucet. It's badly swollen, but that will go down in a few days. You can take a couple of 222s when you need to ease the pain. Come back in two days to have that head wound redressed. And if you have any symptoms of a concussion you need to contact your own doctor right away."

I held out my hand to catch the pills and then he pivoted around on his paper slippers and flew out of the emergency room, lab coat literally flapping in the wind. I guessed I didn't help make his day any easier.

"Here," said Winn and he handed me a plastic baggie filled with cotton-batten rolls. I touched my head and whimpered.

"If you expect me to feel sorry for you, I don't. You're lucky someone called the police."

"Who called?" is what I said, but it came out sounding more like "Ru walled."

Winn interpreted my slurred question accurately. His job would require him to listen to a lot of punched-up drunks.

"I don't know, Ms. Walker, but I have a feeling you do." Suddenly I was so tired I wanted to lie down on one of the gurneys parked against the wall. I felt as if I could sleep for a week.

Winn ordered a policewoman waiting outside the room to drive me home and see that I got tucked in safely, but not before telling me he would arrange a time for another interview when I felt better.

My son, Jon, over six feet tall and built like a rugby player, came to the door the minute the blue and white pulled up to the curb. The police must have called him at school. His number is in my wallet in case of emergency. My mother's number is, too, but heaven forbid she find out any unfortunate information that I haven't already screened. She'd just stare at me and shake her head until I wanted to strangle her.

Jon was in his fourth year at a local college, studying environmental science. His young face was lined with concern. Together the rookie and my boy helped me through the front door and upstairs to bed.

As I eased the covers up to my swollen chin, sinking into the feathery pillows, I could hear them talking downstairs in the hall. She was probably close to the same age as Jon, around early twenties. Halfway to dreamland I heard the pretty rookie giggle.

chapter three

I went back to work Monday morning after taking two days off to recuperate. My head ached and the room tilted sideways if I stood up fast. The chip in my tooth was barely noticeable, but my jaw was still visibly swollen. The painkillers the doctor gave me made me sleep through the nights without waking once. Something I didn't mind at all. Detective Winn called several times only to have my son answer and tell him I was sleeping. Jon kept a tight vigil and although I felt fine, he would shake his head and mouth "NO" whenever the phone rang.

I'd have to postpone any rigorous exercise for a few more days and my regularly planned visit to the gym this afternoon would have to wait. Because I do my own shopping for the restaurant, which includes lifting heavy cases of beer, wine, and liquor in and out of my car's trunk and because my office is up forty steep steps to the second floor, I'm in better shape than if I used a StairMaster.

Unfortunately, my routine of pounding the track at the gym would be missed. With state-of-the-art headphones and a player full of hardcore rhythm and blues, I get so high on endorphins that I should be issued a safety rope. My present condition, incapable of bending over without feeling dizzy, was hardly a recommendation for doing laps around my living room, let alone a mile-long relay.

Most wannabe restaurateurs think you have to work every weekend and evenings in order to run a tight ship. Not really. The restaurant is more likely to fall into trouble on a Monday or Tuesday when the only staff scheduled are fledgling waiters and second-string kitchen help (If for some bizarre reason, like the bus stops here and the place fills up, then heaven help.) The most experienced floor staff and kitchen people work Thursday, Friday, and Saturday, traditionally the busiest shifts, so I leave it up to them to run the show. Invariably, when I do try to help, I somehow manage to get underfoot and shooed out of the way.

The name Walker's Way Bistro was etched with white paint onto a wide expanse of plate-glass window that ran across the front of the building. Other than a band poster stuck to the front door, there was no recent evidence of foul play. The plate glass has had to be replaced so many times in the past that it eventually caused the insurance underwriters to levy an enormous deductible. This was to discourage me from filing any more claims and it worked. One more thing I expected to pay out of pocket. Crazies, bums, and dope fiends sadly have nothing better to do than smash my windows in the wee hours of the night. And in case you're wondering, I am not an egomaniac. I named the place Walker's Way because my last name is Walker and I hate making up names; hence the name Kitty, for the cat.

I unlocked the front door of the restaurant, tilting my head to avoid the drooping steel chain that was attached to the top of it. Using ready-made cement, Rick had secured the other end of the safety cable into the brick surrounding the door. When he first showed me the chain, I asked him what he did with the ocean liner that it belonged to. It was a heavy son of a gun. He explained the chain was guaranteed not to snap (duh, no kidding).

Two years ago, in the height of a nasty storm, the front door flew off its hinges and flipped end over end down the street, narrowly missing a station wagon with Oregon licence plates. I remember Rick running down the street after it and the looks on the occupants' faces that silently screamed, "Toto, we're not in Kansas anymore."

Breakfast was not served Monday through Wednesday for fear of staff mutiny. It was a couple of hours before the front servers would be arriving and the dining room was empty. The kitchen staff was prepping in the back, but they may as well have been on the moon. They came in the back door, left by the back door, and unless they were dying of thirst and couldn't terrorize one of the servers into bringing them beverages, they never ventured out front.

Personally, I would have preferred leaving the front door open, but Rick convinced me locking it was better. Anyone could walk in and steal a tablecloth or even a table, for that matter, but as I tried to tell him, it was highly unlikely that would happen again.

Ultimately, the real reason we locked the front door was because we got tired of finding people sitting at the tables. Heaven only knows how long people have sat there waiting for a menu. Granted, some of our waiters are slow, but if the there's a mop with a bucket of dirty water in the middle of the floor, then — trust me when I say this people — you're not getting one anytime soon.

I could hear the kitchen staff busy preparing for a new week. Most of the desserts, salad dressings, and stocks would have been consumed over the busy weekend and needed replenishing. Without a head chef, there would be a lot more prep than usual.

Before heading up to the office, I took a peek in the kitchen. Rick was talking to a bald man with the beginning of a pot belly who looked to be around forty years of age. He had a firm grip on a black leather briefcase and a cook's knife pouch tucked under his arm, very professional-looking. *Well done*, I thought, wondering where Rick found a replacement chef so quickly. It didn't matter, Rick has his own resources and as long as he was happy, so was I. I wanted to ask what restaurants the man hailed from, but decided not to interrupt while I still had a slightly swollen jaw and a gauze bandage on the top of my head. Wouldn't want to give the new help the wrong impression.

The office answering machine light was blinking. I recognized the caller's name and reached out to play the message back when someone knocked at the door. Detective Winn walked in, took two steps forward, and stopped cold. Surprise, or perhaps it was disgust, crept across his face as he took in the surroundings. I was the first to admit the office was messy and yet somehow I never felt like cleaning it up. Stacks of file folders and paper receipts covered the desk. Tools of every sort, more plumbing parts, plastic totes full of electrical doodads, and a roll of pink insulation dominated one end of the floor. It was a necessary environment of flux and flow that I found comforting.

Instead of artwork, I have ten years of past menus nailed to the walls, a few in frames, and the others laminated. The only similarity between them over the last ten years was the hamburger. Even the Dijon mustard, the only condiment served along with it, was the same. Never fear, ketchup was just a simple request away, with our waiters always happy to oblige. Well not always. I'm told they sometimes lie and say we're all out, but not when I'm around.

Before I finally relented and purchased a deep fryer, the burger was served with potato salad. The salad was good, but not nearly as good as the shoestring fries we serve now. Kudos to the inventors of deep fryers, without which my weekly craving of deep fried calamari would go unfulfilled. One thing the restaurant lacks is a microwave and unless someone buys me out or kills me, it shall remain forever so.

Detective Winn caught me staring at him and he blushed. I thought that that was adorable for a big guy like him and smiled.

He snorted. "Ms. Walker. That jaw looks sore. Maybe you should have stayed off your feet for a few more days."

"I can't rest. Too hyper. I'm lucky to get a good night's sleep when life is normal. With all this excitement, I just hover above the bed. Might as well be at work. Want a coffee? It will just take me a minute." Jeepers, I was chipper.

A small Gaggia espresso machine that was about a hundred years old was kept in the office. It used to be housed in the restaurant, but it'd had its guts repaired so many times that I couldn't afford to repair it anymore. Besides, the original parts, which the importer brought over from Italy fifty years ago, were all used up. I baby it now.

"That would be great, thanks," he replied. "While we're waiting, I wanted to ask you some questions about the business."

I swung a chair around for him, brushing off a few crumbs that were stuck to the seat. "Why, you thinking of getting into it?" I asked. "I think you make a better-looking cop than a maitre'd."

"I'm not sure if that's a compliment or an insult." He blushed again and sat down.

"Neither am I. Sometimes I have no idea what I mean." I cleared my throat, wondering why I was picking on the guy and asked him, "If you're so surprised to see me, then why exactly are you here?"

"I understand Richard Best is the executive manager for the restaurant. I was hoping he could give me some information about Daniel. A resumé could be useful if you still have one around."

I rummaged around in a desk drawer and pulled out a file marked "Chefs." Someone's resumé with the name of Philip Sutherland was on top. Presumably it belonged to the new guy Rick was showing around downstairs. Daniel's was next. I stuck Daniel's resumé in the scanner, made a copy, and handed him the original.

Winn slipped it into his briefcase and looked at me, waiting for goodness knows what. I began wondering if he was single when he finally broke the spell.

"How well did you know Mr. Vieira, the deceased, Ms. Walker?"

"I didn't know him. I saw him sometimes when I was shopping in his store, but never socially."

"Maria D'Agnole was an employee of his. Did you know her?"

"We were acquainted. Is that important?"

"I'm trying to get a background. She was the one who found the packages along with, ah, the other things."

"What other things?"

"Can't give out details as yet. Some things only the killer and the police know."

"How's she doing?"

"Some initial shock was to be suspected. She's recovering at home. I thought you might shed some light on her personality, and while you're at it," he said, leaning toward me in his chair, "I was hoping you might tell me where your chef is."

"I don't know where he is. No one has seen him." It was my turn to lean forward. I leaned forward to meet his gaze, two could play his game. "Why are you asking me about Maria? Do you think she killed him?"

"We're conducting a thorough investigation and your co-operation would be appreciated. If you don't mind …" He pulled out a notebook and read flatly, "Ms. D'Agnole was asked by her boss to open the store that morning as he had a personal matter to see to. A cabbie dropped her off at the rear entrance in the lane behind the store. It was very early, still dark out, and nothing else open in the lane except for the bakery. The driver remembers, 'The smell of fresh bread seeping into the car.' He was worried about her since she was alone and watched her until she was safely inside.

"A homeless man, who bedded down in the store's doorway, heard a scream, and when he looked in the window, saw her lying on the floor inside. Ms. D'Agnole hit her head on the glass display unit when she fainted." He closed his notebook and under his breath I heard him mutter, "I think I would've, too."

The detective looked up and waited for me to speak.

I had nothing. "So?" I said.

"Is it possible your chef was having an affair with Maria?"

"How on earth did you jump to that conclusion?"

"The initials W.W. were written in the victim's own blood. I believe someone was trying to — as they say in the movies — point us in a direction. We are trying to establish a motive for the murder, maybe jealousy."

"I don't think he knew Maria or anyone else from Superior Meats. Daniel left the orders on their answering machine and they were delivered the next day. Since there was a minimum amount required for delivery, I sometimes went in to pick up the odd item. To my knowledge he never did."

"When we questioned the store's staff about your chef, they said they knew you from shopping in there, but didn't recall your chef's name. Yet when we showed them his driver's licence photo, they immediately recognized him. Recently, on separate occasions, he had been seen talking to Mr. Tony in his back office. None of them overheard their conversations or knew what it was concerning. What do you think of that?"

"I have no idea what he was doing."

"One of the staff there mentioned you were on friendly terms with Maria D'Agnole."

"I'm a friendly person. There's a coffee shop next door to Superior Meats where the staff take their breaks. I often grabbed a muffin in there and chatted with the girls. Maria was a little distant with the others, but she was always nice to me. She often sat by herself and I'd join her. We talked a few times over coffee and occasionally in the store when she wasn't being shadowed by her boss."

"Shadowed?"

"Yes, Mr. Tony, as the girls liked to call him, had a thing for her. He was always whispering in her ear. One day I watched him trail his fingers along her spine. The other sales girls saw it, too. It gave me a chill. I've been shopping in there for over ten years and from what I've seen, I think he had a thing for a couple of them. The women are different ages, but Maria was a very young girl when she started at the store, maybe eighteen or nineteen years old."

My thoughts drifted back and I started to remember what Maria had told me about growing up in Canada.

After Maria's mother became sick and died of breast cancer, her father, Roberto, moved his family from Portugal to Canada in search of a new life. Maria was a sad little eight-year-old who spoke no English. Two older sisters battled their way through the Ontario educational system, dropped out as soon as legally possible, and moved away even sooner. Left all alone in a house that their father paid for by working ten-hour shifts, six days a week, Maria was looked after by a young widowed Portuguese girl who eventually became Mr. D'Agnole's second wife.

Loneliness translated itself into sullenness, making Maria appear aloof to others her own age. She had no friends or family and her stepmother, whom she never got on with and who preferred the smaller but airier kitchen on the first floor, left her alone to study in the basement's grotto-styled kitchen undisturbed for hours.

She had been a good student, graduating with honours from elementary school and gliding effortlessly through secondary school. Her father was very proud of his youngest daughter, although she had come along later in life than he would have liked and eventually the stress of raising three daughters in a new country and a new wife's demands took its toll. When he had to cut back on his shifts at the local foundry, money grew scarce and Maria knew she would have to quit school and find a job. Her stepmother mentioned a meat company she used to work for was hiring. Then, as Maria dragged her heels, an application form miraculously appeared in the all saint's alcove at the foot of the stairs. The new Mrs. D'Agnole said she could still pull a few strings.

That was years ago, Roberto's bride had pulled up stakes long ago for a more ambitious younger man. True to tradition, Maria, the last unmarried daughter, moved back into the empty house to care for the broken man he had become.

"She was eighteen," Said Winn, interrupting my reverie.

"What?" I said, startled.

"I questioned Ms. D'Agnole the following day," said Winn. "She was eighteen years old when she started at Superior Meats."

The detective removed his leather jacket, exposing a side arm tucked against his side. He wrapped the jacket around the back of his chair and glanced over at the espresso machine. "How about that coffee? I think it's done."

"I totally forgot, sorry." I jumped up from the desk, teetered a little, and brushed his arm as I moved to get the coffee. The subtle aroma of masculinity jolted my olfactory memory bank. I inwardly groaned.

"Did you say something?"

Well, I thought it was inward. "I was wondering how you take your coffee."

"Black is fine, thanks."

Black was how I liked mine, too. We should get married. I handed him a cup.

"You were saying about Maria?"

"I just told you, beyond chatting a few times, we never spoke. Why do you find that so hard to believe?"

"It looked like you were thinking of something a minute ago. Want to tell me about it?"

I told the detective what I knew about Maria's past and said that was pretty much it.

"She was far more fascinated in my business. She'd ask me all kinds of questions about my staff, their qualifications, or where they were from, and how I found them. I thought perhaps she was interested in starting her own place. She also wanted to know what it was like watching people eat all day long."

He laughed. "What is it like?"

"It's like having a giant dinner party. People are usually happier when they eat. I know I am." I giggled and stupidly patted my tummy to prove it. I quickly added, "Business is business, but the perks in this one are great."

Winn looked around him again and I was pretty sure he wasn't thinking that my office was one of them. The couch against the wall had stuffing leaking from its seams, the ceiling's century-old plaster trim was breaking off in chunks and the original antique porcelain fireplace had a fake electric log in its grate that Rick turned on whenever I got depressed. It was on now.

"Nice fire," he said sarcastically.

"Thanks," I shot back. "It really warms up the place, don't you think?"

Winn answered that with an uncertain nod and asked, "How did you get into the food business?"

"Is that what you came to talk about?"

"I just wondered. Is that all right?" He turned on a smile that knocked my socks off. I cleared my throat a couple of times and tried to explain.

"Well it wasn't a lifelong fantasy, nothing as romantic as that. More like sheer desperation. I was struggling at school and agonizing over an intended career course. During my university years, I was lucky to get a part-time job as a waiter in a small but established Italian restaurant. The owners were an older couple, the epitome of sophistication. They knew everyone in town, politicians, gangsters, professors, and hookers, united under the same roof, peacefully consuming gallons of red wine and shovelling plates of Spaghetti Carbonara down their throats."

Winn chuckled faintly in response to the picture I was painting.

I continued, "Reggie and Betty, the owners, insisted that the staff call them by their first names, allowed us to eat one free meal per shift. The younger employees, especially the students, were always broke. We really appreciated being fed and the food was to die for. Not like undercooked chicken wings with half the feathers still on them."

"You ate that?" Winn asked.

"No, that was the whole point. The owners went away one week end and the chef, who was an ornery old misogynist, decided that was all a bunch of sluts, his pet name for the waitresses, deserved."

"I take it there's a happy ending to this story?"

"Reggie came back earlier than intended and saw us trying to eat the measly wings, feathers and all. He literally threw the chef out the door. You know, life has a funny way of biting you in the ass. My mother always says, 'Be careful of the seeds you sow.' It's true. When I opened my restaurant, years later, the same man came in and applied for a position as head cook. Boy, was he surprised to see me. I told him there was a position as a dishwasher available and he called me a slut. Anyhoo, before that I never ate in a fancy restaurant. I guess without knowing it I kind of absorbed their lifestyle and eventually fulfilled the fantasy."

"I never ate out before I left home either," said Winn. "Good old-fashioned home-cooked meals and apples for dessert. I remember longing for the chance to eat fast food and now that's all I ever eat. Be careful what you wish for too, I suppose."

"Don't feel bad. I thought McDonald's was heaven."

Detective Winn smiled and my heart skipped a beat. However, besotted as I was, I didn't believe for a second he was playing nice because he was interested in me. He was as about as relaxed as a coiled spring. Maybe he knew where Daniel was and he was stringing me along to see what I knew. "Who do you think killed Mr. Tony? Could it really have been Maria? Because I know it wasn't Daniel."

"So you say, but I can't discuss it with you. I can tell you that Ms. D'Agnole was very upset after her unfortunate discovery. She didn't give us any information at the time because she was incoherent with shock. It's hard to fake that. When I suggested that I come to her house for an interview, she insisted on coming to the station instead. Her father had just suffered a massive heart attack and she thought it might upset him. I thought it was a reasonable request."

"That was noble of you," I said.

"Is that sarcasm?" he asked.

"No, I'm serious. I didn't think the police gave a … well, never mind. That was nice of you." I smiled.

"I respect Maria's dedication to her father. In fact, she made me feel guilty enough to call my own mother. I'm going to drive up to see her this weekend."

"Where do they live?" The way this conversation was going, you'd think we were on a date. I figured he was used to manipulating conversations and let it fly.

"My mother lives just outside of the city. She's all alone now — my father passed away this summer."

"Sorry, mine died last spring, too."

"Sorry. I guess they were getting too old."

"I guess we're getting old."

He smiled and said, "You look all right." He sheepishly touched his hand to his thinning hair before continuing, "My father died barbequing steaks in ninety-degree weather. My mother looked through the kitchen window and wondered why there was a stream of black smoke rising from the grill. The same evening she called me at midnight from the emergency ward."

Again, I told him I was sorry and meant it. The moments ticked by and then Winn shifted gears so fast I almost fell out of my chair. He stood up and placed both hands flat on the desk.

"What were you really doing at the exhibition last Friday?" He was all business again.

I pressed my back against the chair, recoiling from him. "I wanted to find Daniel."

"Did you know he was working there?"

"I figured it out when I saw the box of steaks in his trunk marked C.N.E. I had no idea until then. I may not share your level of expertise in such matters, but I had a hunch."

"Do you have 'a hunch' as to where he is now?"

"Nope. I haven't seen or heard from him."

"He is wanted as a murder suspect. If you know anything at all, you'd better co-operate."

He was trying to bully me. A futile attempt considering mine was traditionally a male-dominated business and I got tired of taking crap a long time ago for not belonging to the club. I held my hands in the air for the international sign — *that's enough*. "If you're insinuating that I'm keeping something from you, then you are sorely mistaken. I didn't see Daniel at the exhibition. I just thought I heard his voice. The next thing I knew I was waking up in the hospital."

Winn backed off. "The situation has worsened for Daniel, Ms. Walker. He's in serious trouble."

His warning was real, but how could I help? "I heard there was a case of food poisoning reported at the convention hall that morning. You think he's responsible for that, too?" I asked.

Winn straightened up and held out his card to me. "If you hear anything that will help us with our investigation, Ms. Walker, I want you to notify me immediately, otherwise you can be charged with obstruction."

I jumped out of my chair. He had pushed my buttons. I pushed back.

"First you act all friendly with me, Winn, then you tell me I'm in danger and threaten me. I want to know what's going on."

"That's Detective Winn, Ms. Walker. And I was not acting. I was actually relaxing for a moment. I don't know what came over me."

"Gee, thanks." I sneered.

"I'm not compelled to share police information with you, although you did hear right. The same morning you were knocked on the head at the exhibition, two people suffered severe food poisoning. I believe your attack is connected to theirs, but until I find out why,

I'm concerned about your safety. The names of the poisoning victims will be released tonight. Since you seem to be in danger of having a nervous breakdown, I may as well tell you now."

"Don't patronize me."

"Do you want the names or not?" he asked.

Defeated, I nodded my head. He spieled off the names, "Councillor Stephen Albright and Cecilia Vieira."

"I remember waiting on the councillor at Reggie and Betty's restaurant. He was a regular with the rest of the politicos."

"What was your impression of him?"

"A little short on integrity. I saw him grab a tip off a table once and pocket it. But who's Cecilia Vieira?"

"She's the wife of the late Mr. Tony, a.k.a. Anthony Vieira." He looked at me squarely. "You see how things may be connected." He consulted his little notebook again. "She and the councillor were poisoned while attending a breakfast affair welcoming the show's participants in the executive dining room of the new convention building. Shortly after eating his breakfast of steak and eggs, Councillor Albright complained of a pain in his stomach, stood up and toppled over." He raised his eyes momentarily to get my reaction and continued to read from the page, "After first vomiting on the table in front of her, Mrs. Vieira followed suit. They were rushed to the hospital and prematurely diagnosed with a case of botulism — that's a serious form of food poisoning."

"I think I know what botulism is by now."

"Yes, I guess you would."

My head snapped up to see if he was intentionally insulting me.

"Relax, I didn't mean anything by that. If you will allow me to continue, this case has turned out to be a lot more sinister than a fatal reaction to food poisoning.

Mr. Albright died last night and further investigation by the coroner has determined the meat was spiked with rat poison. We are looking at another murder." He snapped the book closed.

I sat down hard, nearly falling out of the chair when it spun around, and using my feet as brakes, I choked out, "How about Tony's wife? Is she going to die, too?"

"Probably not, she's hanging in there. We don't think she was the intended victim. She ordered scrambled eggs with toast. Apparently she doesn't like red meat after all the years in the business with her husband."

"I know how she feels. I used to love cheesecake and now I can't stand the sight of it. Sorry, not really relevant is it."

The detective gave me a weak smile. "The good councillor convinced Mrs. Vieira to try a piece of his steak, said it would make a good impression, given the theme of the show and her husband's business involvement. A newspaper reporter has given us a publicity photograph he took of her sharing a bite. Good thing she didn't have more."

He finished off the dregs of his coffee, put the cup down, and launched into the final round of badgering. "Now, are you ready to please tell me what were you doing at the Exhibition grounds, Ms. Walker?"

"Read my lips. I went looking for my chef."

"Why? Were you in love with him?"

"Don't be ridiculous."

"Come on, Ms. Walker. He's a pretty good-looking guy. Admit it, were you having an affair with your chef?"

"You thought Daniel was having an affair with Maria a few minutes ago."

"Everyone is under suspicion. Answer the question."

"No, of course not. I will admit Daniel and I were on pretty good terms, but not that good. You have no idea how hard it is find a chef of his calibre."

"It doesn't bother that you that he may be a cold-blooded killer."

"That's ludicrous. He's not a killer. To be honest, I don't care anymore. Rick has already hired someone else."

"I hope that means you'll stay out of my investigation. Two serious crimes have been committed and most likely, given the circumstances, were committed by the same person or persons. You realize I'm serious when I say that you could still be in danger. Someone hit you on the head for a reason. Someone called and saved your life for a reason. And all you're telling me is that you went looking for your chef, hard to believe considering we found you in a Dumpster behind the cattle building."

I didn't know I had been found in a Dumpster, but it certainly explained the grease stains on my clothes. I felt odd, as if having an out-of-body experience. Winn handed me my coffee and told me to take a drink. The umbilical surge of caffeine steadied me.

"What did you see before you were hit?" he asked, quickly forcing my attention back again.

"Nothing, I told you I thought I heard Daniel's voice. It's hard to be sure because of all the noise from the machines running in the background, but there was arguing and someone was shouting threats." I explained. "Maybe Daniel called the police and then ran away."

"The call was made from a cellphone. We've talked to everyone who worked in that area to see who owns one, but it seems they all do."

"Yes. The need to feel in touch. Personally, I hate all phones. The only calls I ever get are ones from the restaurant telling me the toilet is plugged or a cockroach just crawled across someone's dinner."

"You have cockroaches?"

"NO! We don't. An occasional rogue infiltrator perhaps, but that's all." My eyes warned him not to go there.

"You should go home. You look terrible." He slipped his jacket back on and left without so much as a goodbye. I guessed it was too soon to expect a hug. I looked at the card I was holding in my hand. It stated that his office was located in the 51st Division, a modern cellblock of a building not far from the Ontario Art Gallery. The card listed his direct phone number.

chapter four

As soon as the door closed behind him, I pressed the Play button on the answering machine. It was Martin Wright, the waiter I had bumped into at the Exhibition grounds. He said it was important that he speak to me if would I meet him at his apartment around two o'clock. Then he abruptly hung up without another word. According to Martin's employee record, he lived on the other side of town. It annoyed me he didn't leave a message because I had a nagging suspicion it had something to do with Daniel and I didn't feel like driving anywhere.

Back on the Gardiner Expressway, I remembered first to take the Queensway exit in order to connect with Parkside Drive where Martin lived. His street snaked its way north from the lake alongside High Park, one of the largest interior parklands in Toronto. I almost drove to Hamilton once looking for the non-existent exit to the park from the overpass, another fine example of road ingenuity by our forefathers.

Martin lived in one of the tall brick mansions on the hilly side of the street overlooking the park. I had to walk up two steep flights of stone steps, taking an intermission to catch my breath on the terraced landing. Hunched over, I noted with tender admiration the frilly moss growing between the decaying brick's herringbone pattern and decided that I really needed to get back to the gym.

When my normal breathing resumed, I climbed the remaining set of wooden stairs to the front porch. A massive oak door with a glass oval inset was open, leading me to a small vestibule inside. On the door of the main floor apartment were the names Martin Wright and Marshall Lockhart. So Martin and Marshall were roommates. Made sense since they were both waiters at Walker's the same time last year, and from what I heard, they both liked to disco.

Holding my hand in mid-air, I almost rapped Martin on the head when he unexpectedly opened the door and jumped back a foot.

"Hi Marty," I said.

"Oh, my gosh, Liz, you startled me." He was holding a leash with a tiny ball of white fluff bouncing up and down on the end of it. "I was about to take Sammy to the park. I wasn't sure you got my message. It's twenty past two and I have to be at work by three."

I held Sammy's leash while he locked up. The dog jumped at my legs and then tugged me down the steps toward the park. He could probably smell the park through the brick walls, panting by the door until someone got home. Taking the leash back, Martin walked up the street to the pedestrian crosswalk — crosswalks noted for sending out-of-towners into cardiac arrest — pointed with his arm thrust out and crossed with me and the dog trotting closely behind. He turned onto a hardened dirt pathway that led us deep into the interior of the park. We stopped under an aging canopy of rare black oak. Sammy found a bush and I found a bench. Martin refused to sit. He was clearly agitated.

"Sit down, Marty. You're making me nervous."

"I can't. Marshall's mad at me for getting involved. He said I should have called the police."

"Martin, you wanted to see me. Your message said it was urgent. If you were worried about me coming out here why didn't you say what it was about on the phone?"

"I couldn't take the risk someone other than you would listen to the message."

"You can trust Rick. He's the only other person with a key to the office."

"Daniel told me to be careful. He didn't want Rick to know I called. I don't know what kind of trouble Daniel is in, but he was hysterical."

"Please, just tell me what he said."

"He said that he wanted to talk to you. I was busy waiting on tables so I told him to call you at the restaurant. He said he didn't have time — he was leaving town in an hour."

"Leaving town," I repeated. "You had already left Walker's Way by the time he started working there, so how did you know him?"

"I didn't, really. Marshall and I bumped into him in a bookstore on Queen Street a month ago and we got into a heated, no pun intended, conversation about which cookbook to buy. You know how chefs are — so opinionated. He must have seen me talking to you at the show and recognized me. Too cute for words, I must say."

"Martin, what's the message?" I was getting impatient.

"Don't get tetchy." He was stalling.

"I'm sorry. Please continue."

"I don't know what to do, Liz. Maybe I should tell the police." He was staring at his watch.

"Okay, Marty, let's talk about something else for a second. The day I bumped into you at the convention centre, you were starting your shift. You knew your way around the halls pretty good. Did you see something you shouldn't have? Was it you who called the cops to fish me out of the Dumpster?"

"I have no idea what you're talking about and I don't know anything about a Dumpster."

I pointed meaningfully to the bandage on top of my head.

"Or, how you got that nasty bump on your head …" He looked at the fraying bandage on my head and added, "That really does look awful."

I couldn't help picking at the gauze netting with my fingernails and some of the edges had turned a yellowish pus-grey.

He almost begged me, "Would you like me to go back to my place and get you a new bandage?"

I shook my head and smiled, "Forget about it, Marty. Do you know where Daniel is or not?"

"I know where he is, but you have to promise not to tell anyone else."

I raced home, blew the dust off a canvas travel bag kept in the back of my bedroom closet and packed. A raincoat, a pair of black jeans that made my legs look six feet long, two T-shirts, underwear, socks, and a hooded sweat shirt were all stuffed into the bag. I'd be gone only a day or two, but better safe than sorry. I dropped a few toiletries in a side compartment, kept on the slacks I was wearing, smelled my armpits, and pulled on my long, black leather boots. There were enough points logged onto my credit card to make the round-trip free and since I had nothing better to do except worry, I tucked the address Martin gave me into my coat pocket and left a note for Jon in the hall.

It takes two days to drive down east, one, if you decide not to eat or sleep on the way. I promised myself I'd never do either again and I buckled up for the short two-hour flight to Halifax. Despite an inordinate fear of flying, I felt relatively calm.

We flew directly into a full-blown Maritime gale. Coastal headwinds turned the plane into a rocketing bronco ride while booming thunder sent me into near epileptic fits. The student pilot, courtesy Air Canada, announced that we would be landing safely in Halifax in a few minutes. A tad optimistic given the plane was in a nosedive, plummeting to the ground at the speed of light.

"We are making a rapid descent due to the storm," the flight attendant explained. "Quite routine."

"Really," I said, "because my brain thinks it's in a pressure cooker."

I couldn't muster enough saliva to swallow and my sinuses felt as if they had been hot-wired with a glue gun. When the flight attendant, alarmed by my frantic gulping, leaned over my seat, I locked my arms around his neck and held on for dear life. The plane shuddered then calmly levelled out.

"See," he said, pushing the word out through tiny wolverine-esque teeth.

I let go quickly before more spittle landed on my sleeve and handed him a twenty for his trouble.

Grateful to be back on *terra firma*, I practically skipped over to the car rental office. After requesting the biggest car on the lot, the agency loaned me a roomy sedan complete with leather seats that slid all the way back. I'm five foot nine-and-a-half inches in my bare feet and need plenty of leg room or else I start to cramp. I picked up a complimentary Toronto newspaper off the counter and purchased a map from a revolving metal display unit standing next to it. I estimated I had about seventy miles to drive to Portsmith, a little seaside town where Daniel's sister Meriel lived, and where, according to Marty Wright, Daniel was hiding. With one shoe kicked off and the other on the accelerator, I eased away from the rental pad under a late afternoon sky.

I like driving, especially alone. The solitude allows me to replay conversations gone woefully wrong. In my line of business, keeping up an appropriate amount of friendly banter — while remaining tuned in to the operation running at high speed all around me — tends to lead me into conversations where I appear to be a complete idiot. In the car, I imagined how it might have gone, practising future responses for a smarter comeback. I talk out loud and by the time I've worked out all the kinks and arrived at my destination, I'm my old self again — completely indifferent.

Dusk was circling on the horizon, not a night sky yet, but coming fast. The dwindling light played tricks on my eyes and straining to focus on the road, I remembered that few lodgings existed on this wind-swept province. A little-known fact discovered when I was here once before with my son about five years ago. We travelled with a tent and pitched it on a different beach every night to watch the sun set. That was a vacation fondly remembered; this wasn't.

Yesterday, I was slinging elegant hash out of a little corner restaurant, now I was searching for answers to a brutal murder my chef may have committed. Having survived recessions, plagues, global terrorists, and a flood, murder was one more, albeit bizarre, obstacle to hurdle. Luckily, the police didn't think it necessary to give me the cautionary "don't leave town" spiel.

I drove to the edge of the ocean shore and turned off the main highway onto an unlit secondary road. I wanted to drive all the way to Portsmith tonight, but I was bushed. The tension from flying in a hurricane and the long trek from the airport had exhausted me more than I realized. The need to rest was increasing.

The first two motels displayed the cursed NO VACANCY shingle from their welcome sign, a third indicated its establishment was full, too. At this rate, I would be willing to sleep in the backseat. I looked around at the landscape. Grassy fields faded into hilly dimensions on one side, a deepening ocean on the other, and up ahead, the gaping yawn of hell. On second thought, I stepped on the gas, thrusting the car faster through the fog threatening to devour the entire road. A cluster of closed stores popped up suddenly on my left and an old schoolhouse appeared on my right. I stopped the car. A jittery neon sign advertised:

BROWNS SCHOOLHOUSE
HOTEL AND TAVERN

Pulling in, I instantly hit a death-defying pothole cleverly disguised as a puddle. The front end disappeared then bobbed back up with a jolt. I looked around quickly to see if anyone was watching, but there wasn't a soul in sight. I parked the Lincoln carefully between a delivery van and an old fishing lorry, grabbed a couple of bags off the back seat, and scanned the hunchbacked building. A turn-of-the-century brick schoolhouse sat out front with a 1960s-style, four-storey, wooden-slatted addition.The entire building was painted monotone brown. Two deer, silhouetted by the full moon, were grazing in the field behind it.

A salt-studded arrow pointed to the front entrance of the building. Making my way to the battered doors of the old schoolhouse, I could almost hear the recess bell and see the schoolmarm waving me in. The doors suddenly flew open with the strength of a nor'easter. A woman with bright red lips and frizzy blond hair tucked into a chiffon bandana spoke to me in a rapid down-home manner.

"Geez murphy, don't be standing there, by'e, get on inside wit ya."

The doors clanged shut on my heels. Dusty class portraits covered the walls of an oak-lined hallway stained from years of greasy hands and the linoleum floor felt lumpy under my feet. A set of swinging doors sat motionless at the end of the hall. I sniffed the air. Mouth-watering aromas of sizzling beef patties lured me down the corridor. I peered over the doors and stepped into a murky barroom — yahoo, the tavern.

On my left, a woman sporting a platinum wig was working the open grill. Five captain bar stools welded to the front of a horseshoe-shaped counter sat empty around her. Dropping my bag to the floor, I climbed aboard. My eyes adjusted to the lacklustre light while I patiently waited for the cook to notice me. I drummed my fingers quietly on the Formica bartop and watched the large, round clock behind her. Evidently she didn't feel like noticing me. Accustomed to surly cooks, I felt right at home and spoke up smartly, "Hey there, those patties sure smell good. I was wondering who I could see about a room for the night, maybe one of your homemade burgers, too."

"ANDY!" she yelled out while flipping a burger. There were maybe six guys in the whole place and none of them looked up.

"ANDEEE!"

Like magic, a young man appeared by my side, lifting my bag into his burly arms. About six foot four, he was wearing faded blue jeans with the cuffs turned up, a white T-shirt with the Cleveland Browns logo on it, and well-worn shit-kicker boots, the kind where the heels wear down and the toes point up. His hair was combed up into a rockabilly ducktail. All he needed to complete the picture was a pack of cigarettes stuck in his sleeve and a match behind one ear.

"The rooms are forty-five big ones a night," the cook barked, "and if you want something to eat you better tell me now 'cause I close the kitchen early on Monday." I ordered a burger with fried onions, a side plate of fries, and a beer chaser.

Andy, mute until now, spoke to me after I finished my order. "Please, if you will follow me, I will show you to your room. I shall bring your dinner when it is ready."

He had a deep, baritone voice, which, for his size, didn't surprise me, but his deliberate elocution did. Maybe he was practising for a butler's part in the village playhouse theatre.

We went through a rear side door that led us back outside to the parking lot. I checked the Lincoln, gratefully noting that it hadn't been vandalized. When we rounded a distant corner of the building, I sensed there was still time.

The tavern ran the whole length of the first floor. The guest rooms were located above on the upper three floors. Except for the tavern floor, the building looked empty. A second later, a light went on in one of the rooms. Andy noticed it, too, and explained, "We're having the hotel renovated. That's the painter's room. He was having dinner in the bar. He goes to bed early and gets up at dawn so he can get the maximum amount of daylight hours to paint."

We climbed a wide expanse of cedar stairs to a large deck on the second-floor level and continued to a smaller platform at the third. Still going, Andy headed for a metal fire escape that led up to the dormered fourth floor or — if you prefer via wild stretch of the imagination — the penthouse.

"Excuse me. I'm not staying up there, am I?"

"Only floor that's not being painted tomorrow." Andy looked back at me encouragingly. "Don't worry. It's quaint up here and very private. Since no one else is booked tonight, you have the whole floor to yourself."

The Elvis impersonator drew out a ring loaded with keys, unlocked the door and held it open for me. I passed five closed doors on both sides of the long hall, which led into a large panelled sitting room with a timbered arch ceiling and heavily curtained windows. Two table lamps were turned on, leaving dim shadows huddled in the corners.

"Where shall I put your luggage, miss?"

"Ah, you tell me. I don't know which room is mine."

"You can have any room you like, but they're all basically the same, not locked, either, so look them over."

Looking around, I wished I had kept driving. My nerves were on edge enough and this place would have given me the willies even in broad daylight.

"Ah, Andy, is it? How much farther is the town of Portsmith from here? On the map it looks like it might only be about one more hour along the major highway. I was getting tired, but maybe I should have kept going?"

"No, you did the right thing. Eventually you have to get off the highway and follow the coastal road. It's a dangerous drive at this time of night — lots of twists and turns. Besides, the fog makes it a blind drive. Things just pop up out of nowhere."

I recalled the deer behind the parking lot; a flash of hooves on the windshield.

"There's not much in Portsmith. Are you visiting relatives? " he asked.

"Something along those lines," I answered vaguely. I wasn't telling a complete stranger that my chef was a suspect in a homicide and was thought to be holed up there.

"Your food should be ready by now. I shall return presently."

I chose a room with an ocean view beyond the treetops and a washroom next door. I was unpacking my nightgown and storing my toothbrush in a glass by the bathroom sink when Andy returned wielding a tray of high-cholesterol delights and placed it on a coffee table in the main room. The food smelled so good I became light-headed and began fumbling around in my purse for a tip, but before I could fish it out Andy handed me a key from the ring.

"Lock the door after me," he said, scurrying back down the hall. The fire escape door closed behind him with pneumatic hesitation.

With a burger in one hand and a beer in the other, I looked around the large brooding room. I calculated this must be the attic of the old school, used formerly either as a dormitory or a teacher's residence. Some of the furniture was authentically antique, the musty brocaded drapes certainly hinted at it. The tiny bedrooms located in the attached wing must be used for spillover in the summer when the roads are busy again with whale-watching tourists.

I wandered over to a bamboo screen, similar to one I bought years ago in Toronto's Chinatown, standing at the far end of the room. It was weathered with mouse-eaten edges and a faded floral motif that hinted at pink lotus blossoms. A metal door was concealed behind the screen. Knowing I wouldn't sleep unless I checked that it was locked, I turned the handle. The door opened easily onto a well-lit landing with stairs leading down to the lower floors. I looked over the railing and started down. Curiosity was going to be the death of me yet.

The third- and second-floor landings also had metal doors with small inset windows. Both doors were locked and the windows were dark. The tavern floor had two sets of regulation double-hung fire doors on either side of the ground-level foyer. One set flush without handles, no doubt leading to the tavern were sealed tight, and when I pushed down the bar handle on the opposite doors marked EXIT, moist salt air hit my face. I pulled it shut again.

Well, all floors had a fire escape. That was good. The doors opened in an emergency, but locked automatically from behind to prevent access. That was good, too. I didn't need any drunken sailors visiting the penthouse after last call in the tavern. Glad now that I had the wherewithal to jam the empty beer can in the door jamb, I headed back up.

My skin prickled at the second landing. I had an uneasy feeling someone was watching me and glanced toward the window in the door. A figure flitted by on the other side. I raced back up to the fourth floor two steps at a time, kicked out the can, slammed the door, and pushed a chair against the door handle. Couldn't be too sure, I've seen horror movies.

I poured myself a stiff one from the bottle of Scotch I brought in from the car and belted it down. My resolve was crumbling and I sincerely hoped Daniel was worth all this trouble. I spread out the newspaper on the coffee table. The headlines on the second page were hard to miss.

POLICE CONTINUE SEARCH FOR MISSING CHEF
Wanted in Connection with the Brutal Death of Anthony Vieira:

Daniel Chapin, rising star of well known eatery, Walker's Way Bistro, disappeared without a trace. Police are asking anyone with information regarding his whereabouts to call the Hotline number — 416-391-HELP.

At this time, it is unknown as to the extent of his involvement in the mysterious slaying of long-time store owner Anthony

```
Vieira of Superior Meats, a
landmark shopping destination
in Kensington Market ...
```

It was a smaller article repeating the top story published in yesterday's evening news and didn't give any more detail of the murder, pending investigation. It did mention that his wife was left behind, he had no children, and that a closed funeral service would be held tomorrow. The store was closed until further notice.

I searched for information regarding the councillor and Mrs. Vieira and found nothing more titillating than a piece about an ongoing police investigation into the suspicious death of Councillor Stephen Albright. Considering they were dealing with a potentially scandalous situation, I assumed the police were keeping a lid on the facts. Albright had been highly visible in the political arena and I was sure they were warned to get the story right before it was presented to the press.

I still didn't know how Mr. Tony was murdered, but I knew it was committed Friday morning in the wee hours before Maria discovered his body and that the poisoning incidents at the convention centre took place hours later, sometime during breakfast.

I rolled the newspaper into a ball and threw it across the room. When Winn discovered I'd done a disappearing act same as my chef, he'd be furious. He'd find me before long. It's not like I used an alias when I boarded the plane.

One drink led to another and I was half in the bag before I decided to go to bed. I pushed up the windows in my room, and the night sea air entered, cooling my flushed skin. The bed was so soft I instantly fell to sleep.

An hour later, I woke up with the room filled with smoke. I couldn't see a thing but when my eyes adjusted I could see it billowing in steady puffs through the dormered windows. I wondered why the smoke was coming in from the outside. A clammy mist enveloped the bed, cold and wet.

Fog! It was tangible enough to dampen my hair. I forced myself to get out of the warm bed, and, wrapping a bed blanket around my shoulders, tiptoed across the cold hardwood floors to shut the window. I heard a faint click. I should have closed the door to my room, but Andy said the other rooms were supposed to be vacant. I peered into the dark hall. Brain on full alert, ears practically twitching, I listened.

Another click, this time I placed it to the fire door located behind the screen. I had been sure it was locked. Instinctively, I threw the covers over my pillows, arranging them into a body shape, and peeked into the hall again. The chair I had pushed against the door as an extra measure of security was being scraped slowly across the floor. I ran down the hall past the empty rooms toward the same back door I came through hours ago with Andy.

Car beams from the parking lot swept the building, cutting through the fog like searchlights. A man was outlined against the frosted glass window of the fire-escape door and someone was moving through the main room toward me. I was trapped in between.

The light arced away quickly, leaving me swathed in darkness again. I groped my way along the wall and felt an open doorway to one of the vacant rooms. I slipped in and closed the door softly. A faint glow of moonlight filtered through the window, casting a shadow across the floor. To my surprise, it turned out to be another washroom.

Stepping into the shower stall, I wrapped the curtain around me and began shaking like a ninny. Why was I so afraid? I've beaten raging chefs to the ground with wooden spoons and learned enough martial arts to bounce martini drunks out the front door with suitable decorum. This was different. This might be the same guy who tried to stop me once before. I still wore the head bandage to prove it.

I heard a creak in the floorboards and a loud curse from the hall. Once the pillows in the bed were discovered, they'd start hunting. I unwrapped myself and stepped out of the stall. There were sounds of a scuffle in the hallway and I heard heavy grunting. I bolted for the window. Standing on the toilet seat, I could just reach the latch to slide it open.

I started climbing over the windowsill, but before I got my last leg up, a hand clamped onto my ankle. I tried to kick out, but the grip was too strong. I twisted around and took a full swing at the head behind me.

"OW!" Right on the money!

The hand dropped, letting me scurry through the window. The light went on in the tiny bathroom.

"Where are you going, Ms. Walker?"

I recognized that baritone immediately and climbed back in.

chapter five

The luxury car rounded the suicide curves with grace and agility. I have been known to drive like a menace, but this time I was really flooring it. Andy sat, arms crossed, staring straight ahead at the road.

"Come on Andy, I'm sorry I kicked you, but if you're not going to talk to me, why did you come?"

"Somebody had to help you, you're a nervous wreck."

"Let's not get carried away. I appreciate you coming to my aid last night, but I would have been fine."

"Is that why you were climbing out the bathroom window?"

"I didn't know it was you, did I?"

Andy shook his head.

Exhausted and coping with a doozy of a headache, I had pleaded with him to sleep in the adjoining room to mine until morning. I needed the company and I didn't have to ask him twice. I guessed he was used to bunking down in the hotel wherever and whenever he liked.

"I don't understand why you were up there at that time of night. You were in a pretty big hurry to say goodbye to me after you brought up the food. I figured you had the night off."

"I wish," he said. "I take over the bar for Evelyn on Monday nights. She visits her mother in the county hospital down in Baysville. The kitchen is closed, but we serve booze until one in the morning." The careful diction had vanished. "I was finishing up for the night, later than usual because one of the old cronies refused to take last call. While I was pulling out of the driveway, my car's headlights picked out a man on the fire-escape stairs. I thought I better check it out. I pulled around to the front of the schoolhouse and went up the fire-escape stairs, through the tavern door exit. I unlocked the door to your floor to do a security check, but it was blocked. By the time I could get it open you were missing from your room, and, just so you know, the pillows in the bed didn't fool me for a second. When I went into the hall I could hear someone running his hands along the wall for guidance. I crouched down and when he got close to me, I tackled him.

"It could have been me." I protested. His grin faded.

"I knew it wasn't. The light from the fire-escape window outlined a man's figure. My eyes had already adjusted to the light, giving me the advantage; he couldn't see me in the dark. Only problem was, the guy kicked me in the head when he toppled over me and by the time I regained my senses, he was headed back down the fire escape. I turned on the lights and checked the rooms to see if you were hurt, that's when I saw you climbing out the bathroom window."

I thought about that. "After I heard the chair being pushed across the floor, I ran toward the fire escape. Someone's headlights swept the building. If everyone else was gone, and you were already in the stairwell, then who was in the parking lot?"

"That was Evelyn pulling in. The painter called her at home earlier in the evening and left a message warning her that something funny was going on upstairs. She drove back to the hotel as fast as she could, but by the time she got back, it was too late. The painter was locked in his room for the night and since he had to get up early, she didn't want to disturb him."

"I didn't see her downstairs this morning. Where was she?"

"Trying to plead with the painter not to leave."

Andy was right about the road. Deceptively calm bays showed evidence of violent transformation. Timbers dried pale as bone and lobster traps loathed by the sea lay hurled and broken against the rocks. I would have died on this road last night; the fog was impassable this close to the shore.

Portsmith was a tiny picturesque seaside village with streets running north and south of the highway. The speed limit dropped to a crawl and I appreciatively noticed the care and preservation of the old naval buildings. At the general store we asked for directions to Macdonald Street. We were informed it was south of the highway, close, but not right on the ocean. Dazzled by the morning sun glinting off the water's surface, we almost missed the turn for Daniel's sister's street. Farther along at the bottom of the hill, the once-mighty ship-repair docks were busy hauling recreational crafts from the water for winter storage.

Daniel's sister lived in a white clapboard bungalow with blue shuttered windows. Typical of east coast fashion, the postwar house was missing its front veranda. The proliferation of wooden butterflies I understood to a degree, but the lack of front porches across the land had me baffled.

I parked a few houses down the road, leaving Andy sulking in the car. Daniel wouldn't know who he was and I didn't want to frighten him with a stranger the size of a prize fighter. Without a porch to stand on, I had to get on the tips of my toes to ring the bell. The button was still beyond my reach. I knocked rapidly at the bottom of the wooden storm door. I was about to leave when the inside door opened. A woman who could be Daniels's double, except with wild red hair, peered down at me through the storm door glass. With one finger she motioned me around to the back of the house.

Rows of glass bottles strung together composed a fence around the side of the house. As I walked past the bottles, I realized they were kitchen stock bottles in every size and shape, mostly olive oil and exotic vinegars, with a few wine bottles thrown in, a uniquely inventive use of recycling.

Daniel's sister Meriel had the best red hair I'd ever seen. Mine always faded after five washes and I told her so.

"It isn't dyed. I just touch up the grey with henna now and then," she said curtly.

"Sorry, I don't want to start off on the wrong foot. I appreciate you seeing me. May I come in?" I asked.

Meriel moved back from the door and I stepped into a rear storage area off the kitchen. The family resemblance was overwhelming. She had the same sinewy build and heavy-lidded eyes as her brother. It made Daniel look sexy; it made her look tired.

"Must be pretty important for you to come all the way out here to see Daniel," she said and then her hand flew to her mouth as if to stop the words.

"So he is here. I must talk to him," I said urgently.

I heard a noise come from the front of the house. I pushed past her, but by the time I made it out there all I saw was Daniel's back disappearing through the front door and jumping out of sight. I reached the door in four steps, ready to plunge after him, but Daniel hadn't hit the ground. Cradled in Andy's arms, he was wiggling around trying to get loose.

"Nice catch, Andy."

"Not much bigger than an ocean tuna," he boasted. "I've caught bigger fish than him before."

"Yeah, well catch this!" yelled Daniel and stuck his finger in the big boy's eye.

Andy dropped him like a hot potato and was about to pull one of the bottles from the homemade fence, when I stepped in between.

"That's enough, you two. Get up, Daniel, and tell me exactly what's going on?"

Before Daniel could utter a word, his sister Meriel, standing at the porch less doorway, announced blithely, "Come on in everybody. Soup's on."

A round table made from burnished oak and set with four brightly woven placemats faced an open window overlooking two neighbours' yards and the distant sea. Minutes later, I was oblivious to the view, happily slurping soup from a white porcelain bowl. "This is the best lobster bisque I've ever eaten," I exclaimed. "Is this where you get all your great recipes from, Daniel?"

Meriel beamed from ear to ear. "Actually, we learned how to cook from our mother," she confessed. "She had a small diner in Halifax for a few years and our father was a fisherman. He supplied fresh fish and my mother made heavenly seafood dishes. Her specialties were bisques of every imaginable kind. This is my favourite, a shrimp and lobster combo. Guess what she called the diner?"

I shrugged my shoulders, too busy soaking up juicy chunks of lobster with thick slices of homemade bread.

"The Sea Biscuit," she announced with a smile.

I was about to fake a gagging sound, but remembered I'd already insulted her hair.

"That's so cute," I said, meaning really corny, but who was I to judge. The chowder was amazing. The mood had lightened and I wanted to keep it that way. Mind you, Daniel and Andy had a few grievances to work out. They were staring at each other like Zulu warlords.

I explained how I met Andy while staying at Browns Hotel the night before and how he had kindly volunteered to drive along to help navigate the coastal road. Nobody questioned his motives. Either this was a friendly custom in these here parts, or both had something else to occupy their minds. Meriel recalled staying at the hotel years ago with their parents to attend a family reunion. It was a fine old hotel that she recalled with fond memories. I was plenty sure I was never going to use the word "fond" to describe my stay. This wasn't a social call and after lunch I told them about the brutal murder of Anthony Vieira. The part about the neat butchering of his body parts made his sister blanch, but Daniel didn't flinch.

"The police want to talk to you, Daniel. You were the last person to talk to Mr. Tony alive. The store's answering machine recorded you saying 'Tony' before it shut off. They think you murdered him. Your fingerprints were all over the place."

"I didn't kill him. I found him like that."

"Why take a runner, then? It makes you look guilty."

"Guilty of what? I couldn't do that to someone! It was disgusting. I ran out of there and called my sister. She told me to come home immediately."

I stole a glance at Meriel. She bowed her head and explained, "I know my little brother and he was terrified. I couldn't fly out to Toronto right away, so I told him to come home."

"You should have called the police first, Daniel. And what about the rotting meat I found in your car trunk?"

"I was going to come back to dispose of it in a few days. It was cool outside so I left the garage door open, hoping the smell would filter away. I didn't want the neighbours complaining."

"Your neighbours are the last people you should be worried about. The police were with me when we found the meat."

Daniel put his head in his hands and closed his eyes.

"Martin, the waiter from the convention, gave me the message that you wanted to talk to me. I flew out here as soon as I could. I hope you appreciate it more than you're acting. If you turned yourself in voluntarily maybe you could come back to work." I touched his arm gently. "Why did you try to run away from me just now?"

He lifted his head, gave Andy a dirty look, and said defensively, "I was keeping watch out the window. When you drove by, I saw you weren't alone. I figured you brought the police."

"Why would I do that?"

"Because you think I killed Tony, don't you?"

"I don't know what to think. First Mr. Tony was murdered and the next morning his wife was poisoned. A city councillor by the name of Stephen Albright was with her at the convention centre and he was poisoned, too. I was attacked while searching for you and I'm not the only one who thinks it's an awfully big coincidence that you were working there as head chef and then suddenly quit."

"I quit the day before. I only went back to get my knives and then heard about the food poisoning that morning. I don't know why you were attacked, but I'm glad you're okay. I don't know who's responsible. Why am I a suspect?"

"Because you keep popping up where dead people are concerned ..."

"Dead...?"

"The councillor wasn't as lucky as Mrs. Vieira. Albright died last night. They think it was from the same batch of meat they found in your trunk."

"That's impossible. I called Tony at Superior Meats after I closed Walker's kitchen. I was supposed to meet him, but his machine picked up and before I could say anything except his name, the line disconnected. I figured he hung up on me so I went over there."

"What time was this?"

"Around midnight, when I pulled down the alley, the bay door was open. Several cardboard cartons marked for the C.N.E were stacked in the doorway and one whiff told me they were the steaks I was supposed to deliver to the show in the morning. I loaded my trunk as fast as I could. I wanted to hide them from Tony. I hadn't figured out how I was going to tell him I couldn't go through with the plan."

"Whoa, what plan?" Andy blurted out. My eyes told him to be careful.

"It was Tony's idea. He wanted to give food poisoning to the guests of the new Spring Fair."

"Food poisoning!" Andy cried. "You got to be kidding me. That's the dumbest plan I've ever heard of."

I kicked him hard under the table.

Daniel ignored the outburst. "I thought Tony was kidding. He was the boss, after all, so I went along with the joke. I was putting in a lot of hours, late at night, setting up menus for the various events and it wasn't unusual for him to hang around and have a few drinks. Then one night he showed up roaring drunk. He kept repeating that he would 'get even.' And, if I helped him, he'd pay double what he owed me."

"What did he want you to do, exactly?"

"Serve tainted meat at the opening ceremonial brunch."

"Wouldn't someone notice?"

"Not if you marinated the steaks overnight in garlic and wine. There might be a hint of an odd taste, but nothing more. By the time the cases in the trunk were found though, they would have been too far gone to mask the smell. "

"That's why you went over to the store."

"Yes."

"You didn't see Mr. Tony?"

"Not exactly. Listen, I wasn't going through with it, I was just pretending to. My reputation would be on the line if I was caught and I'd never work in the industry again. Tony didn't care. He was hell-bent on it and I never saw him like that before. I don't know what got into him, but I was throwing the steaks out and if he tried to stop me I was prepared to fight. Only he didn't come back out of the store, which was strange, especially with his rear cargo doors open and considering he was already mugged in the alley years ago."

"How did you know about that?" I asked.

"Everyone knew. He was terrified of it happening again. He used to work in his office after everyone had gone home. He counted the receipts for the day and dropped the cash in the bank's night-deposit box. I guess he thought he could handle himself until one night he was jumped. He was a cocky son of a bitch, shoving people around. He thought he was tough. Whoever it was taught him a lesson. He was found the next morning locked in the trunk of his car. Besides being robbed, he was pretty shaken up. He had an expensive alarm system installed and bought a safe for the office."

I reminded him of the restaurant safe and how it was a magnet for thieves. The tension in his eyes eased for a second and he laughed. He knew there was never any money in it. I always borrowed a twenty from one of the staff's cash envelopes before I left for the day and Daniel had personally loaned me out of pocket a few times.

Superior Meats would be different. They didn't take credit cards and had a minimum purchase for debit. I've seen a lot of cash exchange hands while waiting to pay for my purchase. Any safe of theirs would be full and consequently a prime target for thieves."

"So you loaded your car and then what?"

"Something was wrong. I could feel it in my bones. I walked along the hallway that connected the delivery area to the showroom up front. The overhead lights were off, but the blue fluorescent tubing inside the display case cast a glow, so it wasn't completely dark. Except for the compressors kicking on and off, the place was deathly quiet. I didn't want to call out. I can't explain it, but I was afraid of disturbing someone or something.

"I found an open carton of packages on the work counter behind the case. The letters W.W. were written across the front of the box. I wondered what it was doing there since I never placed an order that night. I picked up one of the packages and turned it over. A gooey liquid seeped through the paper and covered my hands. When I smelt my fingertips I instantly recognized the odour." Daniel hesitated.

"Blood." I finished his thought.

"Yes. Lots of it and bright red. I remember being surprised at the colour. It had to be a fresh kill for that texture of blood and I knew Tony didn't slaughter on the premises. Suddenly I got the feeling I wasn't alone. There was someone else in the room."

I held my breath, waiting.

"A face was looking at me through the display case. I was scared, but I couldn't look away." His breathing had become rapid, his eyes unclear. I waited. We all waited.

"You know how sometimes you have to focus really hard to understand what you're seeing?" Daniel continued, "Like the picture doesn't make sense. I stepped closer and finally understood. The face had been peeled off and the skin stuck on the inside of the glass in its own blood. When my brain finally clicked the image into place, I panicked. I looked around, desperately trying to put it together. Then I saw the severed head sitting on a scale. That did it! I dropped the packages, ran down the hall, and slammed the door behind me. I'll never forget that narrow screen flashing the weight in pounds and kilos over and over again."

I gave him a moment and asked quietly, "Then what did you do?"

"I drove directly home with the meat in the trunk. I was too scared to do anything else but hop a plane to see my sister. It was awful, such a lot of blood." Daniel's hands began to tremble. Meriel put a steadying hand on her brother's shoulder. Andy reached over and put his hand on mine. Nervously, I withdrew it.

"Daniel, you weren't the only one to witness that gruesome scene. Maria D'Agnole found Anthony Vieira's body when she opened the store in the morning."

"Who's that, their cleaning lady?"

"You don't know her? She worked as a sales girl in the store. Young, black hair, very pretty."

"No, sorry, I made it a point to stay away from the girls. Tony was bossy and possessive around them, always flirting. I didn't want to get involved." Daniel's eyes drifted away and he began to whine, "I put all the spoiled meat in my trunk. I know it. Something else must have caused the food poisoning. Maybe the eggs were spoiled."

"Andy, let's get one thing straight, okay? It was not food poisoning that caused Albright's death. He ingested a lethal dose of rat poison that was injected into his steak. The police are calling it a murder, not accidental death. Tony's wife is in the hospital being monitored as we speak. She ate some, too."

Andy stared out the window at the view. I followed his gaze. White caps swelled along a range of mountainous waves.

"I don't know anything about rat poison." Daniel had calmed. Here was a man solaced by the sea. Born and raised in the Maritimes, he would naturally find comfort in the raw elements. He must miss it living in the city. I knew it would be a few days before I returned to normal. It was would be hard to forget such compelling beauty.

"I warned you to stay away from that man," his sister spoke suddenly. "You never should have got involved with him in the first place." What appeared to be a fresh, homemade, double-layered chocolate ganache cake hovered in her hands midway over the table. She was shaking so much I feared she would drop it. A pot of coffee brewed on the stove, filling the air with heavenly aroma and it was all I could do to stay focused on the conversation. My eyes followed the quivering cake with puppy-dog devotion.

"You hated Tony Vieira," she said. "In fact, whenever I visited Toronto, you refused to go to the market in case we bumped into him."

"All that changed last month when he came around to the back door of Walker's with a proposition. He wanted to bury the hatchet." Daniel gulped. "I mean, make things up to me. I was making news in the food industry and he was looking for someone with my talents. He said he had an opportunity I couldn't turn down. I would be hired to manage the entire food concession for a new spring fair that was opening in the convention centre. I would be executive chef in charge of overseeing menus and ordering. It would be great for my portfolio and the money would be double what I'd make at Walker's in a month. No offence, Liz."

The cake was lowered to the table and placed directly in front of me. Meriel, sensing my inert neediness, cut out a generous wedge and handed me the first piece.

"No offense taken, Daniel," I mumbled, waving a loaded fork around, "and none to you, because I would have thought a chef with more experience would be required to head up an operation of that magnitude. There's a lot more involved than just cooking up pots of soup."

He bowed his head. "I'm afraid my ego got the better of me. I should have known it was too good to be true. All the ordering was done through Superior Meats, but I saw nothing wrong in that. I knew he bid out the contract and that's commonly the practice. With the councillor's connections, he could be looking at a lot of extra business, high-end corporate affairs that might change the structure of his own supply operations. His wife was something else, though. She constantly egged him on to expand his career. Mrs. Vieira thought it beneath her having a glorified butcher as a husband."

Daniel pushed his cake away.

"Any idea what prompted the binge?"

"There was gossip. From what I heard that he finally found out his new buddy was having an affair with his wife. I knew something had to be going on. Why else would a guy like Albright be hanging around the market?"

"He was the elected spokesperson for the Kensington riding. It was only natural," I replied.

"He wasn't too interested in the community. I have friends who live in the market and according to them, none of the residents' suggestions or concerns were acted on, and numerous complaints about rising crime and business loss were also ignored. No one understands why he ran for office last term. If his rival hadn't gotten sick, Albright would have probably lost the election. Even so, he only won by a few votes and that was with full support from Tony."

"Did you ever wonder if Tony may have been responsible for the rival's timely illness?" I asked.

"After I got to know him better I did."

"And why would Albright be ruined and not Tony? Couldn't the meat be traced back to his company?"

"He had it all planned. He bought several cases of sirloin from another supplier. By the time the Ontario Food inspectors had completed their analysis and traced the origin, the convention would be over and the damage would be done to the councillor's good name. It was his responsibility to see that the show ran smoothly. It was his baby. He talked city council into hosting the cattle show in addition to the traditional Royal Winter Fair, which would follow later next season. He volunteered to organize the show to prove his dedication to the project. And if the authorities investigated the source of the problem, which nowadays they most certainly do, then Tony would make sure the finger pointed at Albright."

"I didn't think politicians usually got personally involved with the food handlers. Why would he look bad?"

"As chairman, Albright was able to grant Superior Meats the contract to supply every food operator in the convention building with product. That included booths, restaurants, and staff meals for four days and three nights. In return, he got a share of the sales commission. Not bad for over a thousand pounds of meat and considering the price per pound Tony would charge, the mark-up would be ample. I don't think he'd want anyone to know he fixed the contract."

"How much money are we talking about?" Andy asked.

"A lot. Tony's company would provide bacon and sausages for breakfast, cold cuts, hot dogs, and hamburgers for lunch, plus expensive specialty beef cuts for the big sit-down dinners. At 300 percent mark-up they could split thousands of dollars."

"Also," I added, beginning to agree with his theory, "more important than the money, don't forget the honorary position Albright held. I'm assuming he would be in attendance for most of the meals and so would the press. If he was starved for publicity, like most politicians, this show was a means to enhance his public figure. He could use the success of the show to gain public support. A lot of dignitaries would be in attendance on the opening morning. Albright's future was at stake."

Daniel hung his head. I didn't want to push him and looked around the kitchen. Compared to the small, pristine, formal living room he tried to run from earlier, this room was spacious, warm, and well-used. A full pantry was tucked under an old staircase that probably led to the bedrooms upstairs and a wall of dried herbs and flowers filled the shelves of a gigantic yellow painted hutch standing against the wall. The kitchen cupboards and counter were old and needed refinishing, but the appliances were state of the art. An eight-burner Garland double oven stood at one end of the room and a side-by-side, glass-fronted commercial reach-in refrigerator stood kitty-corner to it. This woman liked to cook. Our simple but exquisite meal was proof that she could.

Finally, I said, "This is serious business. Someone killed Mr. Tony and tried to murder his wife, too."

Daniel looked as if he might jump out the front door again.

"Calm down," I told him. "Whatever you tell me you are going to have to tell the police. Better organize your thoughts now."

chapter six

Andy helped Meriel with the dishes and I helped Daniel pack his bags. Upstairs in his sister's guest room, he concentrated on the task at hand without looking at me. He had more to tell, I was sure of it. When we returned to the kitchen he asked us all to sit down at the table.

"Remember Twister's?" Daniel asked his sister.

"The first place you worked as chef?" Meriel asked.

"Yeah, I was taking over for a previous chef who had disappeared without giving notice. I didn't know that the guy had been buying large orders of beef from Tony Vieira for a kick-back and neither did the owner. First week on the job, I accepted a free prime strip loin, thinking it was a promotional gift. I guess that sounds unbelievably naive, but I was new to Toronto and I'd heard about freebies offered to chefs as giveaways. I didn't know anybody in the trade. A lot of chefs have their own sources and I needed time to build my own. I thought he was legit."

"So what happened?"

"The owner asked me to order from another supplier because the food cost was too high compared to sales. When he showed me the monthly statement for our meat. I saw we were being overcharged on our deliveries. I told Tony I had to cancel that week's order and he got nasty. He threatened to tell the boss I'd been accepting bribes."

"He attempted to blackmail you?"

"You can call it that, but I thought he was bluffing and everything seemed fine until a month later when the boss did fire me. I never planned on staying long at Twister's so it didn't break my heart — it was more bar scene than dining room. Basically, my job was flipping burgers for drunks. After that I worked in various restaurants and clubs around town with Tony always at my heels. Then he disappeared from my life. A couple of years passed and I got hired at Walker's Way, only to find out that you bought from his outlet in the market.

"I was worried about dealing with him, but he never threatened me again. In fact, he seemed to have settled into the role of successful business man instead of a sleazy hustler. I thought I could handle him by now, anyway. I wasn't a kid and I figured you were too established to take any crap. I loved working at your place, Liz. You appreciated my cooking and I had the hots for you, in case you hadn't noticed."

Andy slid his chair closer to mine and Daniel continued his story with his sister shaking her head the entire time. This wasn't helping to improve the atmosphere so I took her hand and smiled.

"Meriel, I've heard of these things happening before. It just takes one rotten apple to spoil the basket." I felt ridiculous spouting food clichés. I tacked another way. "Let's try to stick together on this." I turned to Daniel. "You never mentioned a thing to me about the job at the exhibition."

"I tried to tell you a hundred times, but you were always raving about my food and I didn't want you to think I was abandoning you. I was doing this after my shifts at Walker's and on my days off. I was going to trade shifts with Michael once the show started. Rick knew all about it and said not to worry you."

"Well, I must remember to fire Rick when I get back."

"No, come on, Liz. Rick would do anything for you. He said you were preoccupied with a ton of paperwork and didn't need to know. I said it would only be a couple of days and I'd be back before you missed me."

It's true, I was overwhelmed with figures and cost charts and the feds were breathing down my neck, looking for corporate yearly statements that I hadn't completed for the last five years. Occasionally chefs moonlight. Catering jobs, television spots, and restaurant openings went hand in hand with making a name for yourself. As long as their shift was covered and no sabotage expected, then I really didn't mind.

"Daniel, it's time we headed home. You can explain the rest to the police."

I asked Meriel if I gave her some cash, could I use the phone to call Toronto, but she handed me the phone, dialled the number, and said she wouldn't take a penny. I finally got a hold of Detective Winn at the number on his business card. I called Rick, too. He answered after five rings. I thought I would have to leave a message when he picked up.

"W.W. World Headquarters," he answered.

I've been listening to that for years and it usually made me laugh, not tonight.

"Hi Rick, it's me."

"Where are you? That policeman you're in love with is looking for you."

"I am not in love with him. He's not my type."

"Everyone's your type. Now, where are you?"

"I'm at Daniel's sister's house, here in Nova Scotia."

"You didn't think to tell me you were going on a trip?"

"I'm sorry, Rick. It was a last-minute decision. I'll tell me you all about it when I see you. I'm coming home tonight if I can get a flight. Thanks for holding the fort. Gotta go."

"No, wait. I'm not finished."

"Sorry, I'm not paying for the long distance charges. See you soon, bye." I dropped the phone before he could say another word. To be honest, I hung up because I didn't have the strength to pursue the conversation. Rick could be a real mother hen when he wanted to be and no doubt he already had enough on his hands at Walkers without a chef and an absent employer.

I dropped Daniel and his sister off at a small airfield used for mail and passenger shuttle flights to Halifax. Meriel decided she would accompany her brother to Toronto. I thought it would look better if I flew back with them and delivered Daniel safely to Winn. Andy agreed to return the rental car for me. I tried to board the plane, but it only held six passengers and the seats were filled. The pilot said I could sit in the back with the mail because it was only a short trip and there was an extra seat belt and fold-out chair for emergencies. I peered inside and decided I wasn't boarding a plane the size of an overcrowded soup can. I'd rather go over Niagara Falls in a barrel.

Evening was again on top of us as Andy and I retraced our route back along the coastal highway, only this time Andy drove. He steered the Lincoln through fog patches so dense I feared for our lives. Just in case we crashed through a guard rail toward the briny deep, I gripped the door handle tightly ready to jump out in midair. In retrospect, the soup can looked downright appealing.

We were headed for the hotel until Andy telephoned his boss Evelyn and she told him to take the night off; one of the part-timers had already picked up his shift.

Andy persuaded me to stay over at his place. It wasn't hard. I didn't feel like a long drive back to Halifax. My head still hurt a little and I hadn't got much sleep at the hotel. It was settled. I would return to Toronto in the morning.

Unlike Meriel's place, which was few blocks from the sea, Andy's house sat at the ocean's edge at the top of a small bluff. We arrived around nine in the evening, too dark to see anything from the cedar deck that stretched across the back of the two-storied building. A scalloped trim around a protective awning ruffled slightly in the wind. An odd assortment of furniture and lamps filled the deck, creating an outdoor sitting room. It was very cozy and inviting. I liked it.

He asked me if I wanted to see the ocean, but before I could answer truthfully that all I wanted to do was to lie down on one of the puffy couches, he took my hand and pulled me across a damp lawn to a small promontory platform. I could smell fish and tasted salt on my lips. It was a moonless night and except for the faint flash of a wave's crest, I couldn't tell where the ocean and the sky parted. Andy reached around behind my back and pulled a switch on a pole set into the ground railing. A brilliant white beacon cut across the waves. Inside the streaming alley of powdery light, the foaming curls of heavy green water seemed to rush toward us with malicious determination. Outside its path was oblivion.

I shivered and yawned at the same time, prompting Andy to put an arm around my shoulder and one under my legs. Laid out on an old pullout covered with a heavy duvet and feathery pillows, I watched him remove his boots and then his shirt until he turned off the deck light. Darkness and the smell of the ocean slid over me.

chapter seven

I landed at Pearson Airport around noon the next day and took a taxi home. I refreshed myself with a shower and a nap, washed a stack of crusty dishes that my son conveniently managed to overlook, and drove back downtown. The sun was setting when I rolled into the car park across the street from Walker's Way.

Rick was standing out front on the sidewalk, having an animated discussion with Marlene, one of our waitresses. She was waving a cheque at a person being lifted by paramedics into the back of a waiting ambulance. I ran across the street.

"Marlene, stop it please," Rick was pleading. "The guy has an oxygen mask on his face. What do you want him to do? Tell them to wait while he pays his bill?"

"Well, I'll tell ya, that's one way of skipping out on a bill. He stiffed me, too," she complained.

"Gee, maybe he was too busy dying to think about leaving a tip."

"I hope you don't expect me to pay for his dinner. It's not my fault, ya know. He didn't mention having any allergies."

As conscientious operators, we did our best to scrutinize all the labels on the dry goods for derivatives of nuts and dairy lurking in the ingredients, but some of the more exotic foods were too vague or the English translation too poor for us to decipher. I hoped the restaurant wasn't liable.

Rick's face was turning bright red. I jumped in. "Don't worry about it," I said, plucking the bill out of her hand.

The computer print-out indicated that our hastily departed guest had the New York sirloin entree. The potatoes were hand-cut fries and the pepper steak was served with fresh garden vegetables, roasted with garlic. Nothing on that plate contained nuts or dairy.

I was getting a strange feeling in my stomach. Like fruit flies in a beer bottle. "What else did the man have, Marlene? Bread and butter, cream with his coffee, what?"

"He had the herbed foccacia before his dinner, no butter or oil with it, and a black coffee afterwards. He seemed fine, when all of sudden he started vomiting and blacked out." I looked through the front window and realized the remaining customers needed quick attention. They were wandering around like they had lost their mommy.

"All right, Marlene, back to work. You won't have to cover his bill and have an extra glass of wine on me later as a treat." She ambled toward the bar and I had the feeling she planned on drinking her wine before quitting time. I felt sorry for her tables. She was the slowest waiter on the planet and this episode wasn't going to help them any. Rick comped drinks at all the tables and business returned to normal.

Women customers usually forgave Marlene for her inept service because she was quite young and probably reminded them of their daughters. The men cut her slack because she was quite sexy and reminded them of something else.

She was nobody's fool, though. A customer sitting on the patio, disappointed when he couldn't get her telephone number after asking for repeated coffee refills, complained loudly for all to hear that his saucer was dirty and needed to be replaced immediately. Marlene, having a full section at the time and naturally behind in her orders, walked over to him and picked up the offending saucer. Holding it high in the air, she looked at it in the sun and said, "Ya know, you're right, it is dirty," and flung it over the patio wall into the street. "There," she said, "now it's broken, too."

I chuckled at the memory and walked through the restaurant to the only seat available, the last booth in the back, number nine. Rick slid in opposite me. He told me that Philip, the new chef, was breaking in nicely. Hurray, that was one thing I didn't have to worry about. I felt like having a simple lunch and chose a watercress and roasted pine-nut salad accompanied with a cool glass of sauvignon blanc. Rick and I discussed menu changes for a while and were contemplating going upstairs to the office to do some paperwork when Marlene came over to the booth and whispered, "We might have to close."

"No, no. The customers have settled down," Rick answered. "I bought a round of drinks. Everyone is happy."

Bending closer so that he was forced to look down her shirt, his one eye caught me watching, and he shrugged. Marlene stood up straight, and with arms folded across her chest, she said pointedly, "That's the problem. The chef thought he was entitled to a few drinks, too."

Rick and I floored it into the kitchen, neglecting to use the magic word "IN" and collided with the dishwasher carrying a stack of plates on the other side of the swinging door. Rick caught the plates in mid-air, all except one, which crashed to the floor. He handed them back to the dishwasher, who hurried through the door, yelling, "OUT!"

I scanned the room. "Where is he?"

"Down here," answered Manuel. The salad maker popped his head around the island and signalled with his thumb at the floor. Rick found Philip lying on his back, wedged in between the two Garlands.

"Wake up you syphilitic piece of shit!" Rick hissed and dragged the chef by his feet safely away from the hot oven door and over to the sinks where he dumped a pot of cold water on his head. Clutching his impressive knife pouch tightly against his chest, the bobble-headed chef was escorted out the back door by Manuel. His briefcase was tossed out a few seconds later. Rick finished the standing orders on deck, but things weren't going well. The fruit flies in my stomach were starting to multiply.

Rick was taking stock of the damage Philip had left behind when Marlene came rushing through the door with trouble spelt across her face.

"What could possibly be wrong now?" I shrieked.

"The health inspector is here."

I was not in the mood to grovel. I turned on my heel and slipped out the back door, mouthing the words, "Good luck, Rick." He got paid good money and so far this week all I got was misery.

At home, I waited for Winn to return my call. He didn't, and I fell asleep with all my clothes on.

Usually, about now, a late afternoon lunch crowd would be settling their tab, either returning to the office or heading home. Not today. The dining room was empty. The chairs were stacked upside down atop a row of bare tables with sudsy rings from a recent mopping encompassing the bases below. Back in the kitchen, Rick and a couple of the prep boys were busy emptying the refrigerators.

"Here give us a hand. We're transferring everything to the freezers."

"Are we out of business?"

"No. We've been shut down. The health department gave us a red yesterday."

"Why didn't you call?"

"What could you do? You looked beat. The boys and I are taking care of the perishables."

"Was the inspector unhappy about the leak in the men's washroom?"

"No. He was unhappy about the old guy that was wheeled out of here yesterday."

"That was fast."

"The hospital filed a report as soon as the ambulance took him into emergency. He wasn't allergic to anything and he didn't have a heart attack but he was suffering from a severe case of food poisoning, possibly E. coli, but they're not sure. Unfortunately, this means until the bug and the source can be determined, we can't reopen. Ever since Walkerton, they won't risk an outbreak. They'll get in touch as soon as the lab has finished its analysis." Rick held out a box of thawed shrimp to me and I shook my head no, too much cholesterol.

"I'll take it," Manuel piped up.

Rick handed him the box. "Happy shrimp fest."

I sniffed the air. "What's that smell?"

"The putrid stench of insolvency in the air?"

"Sooo not funny, Rick."

He ran his fingers through his eighty-dollar haircut. "I don't know what it is. I think it's coming from the men's washroom. The urinal is plugged again."

"Man, it just gets worse by the second, doesn't it?"

"This business with the health department doesn't bode well, Liz. Tied in with Mr. Tony's murder and our chef's disappearance, everything seems to be pointing at us."

In Ontario, all restaurants are subject to rigorous health inspections that make me weak in the knees. I swear some of the inspectors are bipolar, intent on working out obsessive-compulsive germ issues and making ridiculous recommendations even hospitals would have trouble fulfilling. Restaurants spend a small fortune keeping up with the demands. Small laminated signs in three different colours: green representing a pass; yellow, a conditional pass; and red, take a pass, are to be displayed in a prominent place for all patrons to see. I came through the front door without noticing the red sign, but that didn't mean our eagle-eyed customers would miss it.

"There are two boxes full of goods that can't be saved," Rick continued. "I told the staff they could divvy it up between them if that's okay with you. Plus, there's nearly full pan of tiramisu we need to get rid of. I've eaten so much of the stuff I can't even look at it." He asked me if I wanted to take some home. Secretly, I still loved the creamy dessert and if he and Manuel hadn't been staring at me, I would have plunged in my face and licked the pan clean. Instead, I gave a thumbs-up to give it to the salad boys.

Rick wore a long rubber apron over his clothes. Always neatly turned out, he wouldn't want to spoil his fine clothes while sorting through the kitchen goods. Since we were closed, he chose to dress down in a pin-striped cotton shirt, a V-neck black cashmere sweater, and pressed blue jeans. He had his own bizarre idea of casual dress apparel. When acting as maitre'd, he preferred wearing a dark Armani suit with a fresh rose in his lapel. He adhered to the theory that a first impression is a lasting impression. I thought he looked overdressed for a casual style bistro like Walker's, but nothing would sway him. As I often commented about Rick, he was oddly consistent and consistently odd.

Rick had a quirky sense of devotion to the restaurant; one that scared me a little. He was personally scarred by a poor review or slow week of business. "It's the beginning of the end," he would announce repeatedly until the customers started to roll in. And heaven help the inconsiderate nincompoop who made a large reservation and didn't show up.

Rick kept a table for twenty reserved on a busy Friday evening, turning away potential customers only to realize too late that the reserved party wasn't coming. After particularly slow nights and a year later, he still calls the inconsiderate party's telephone number to inform them their table is ready and then hangs up. I told him he better be careful they didn't call the police for harassment and have the calls traced back to him.

"Impossible," he explained. "I buy disposable cellphones from the drug dealer on the corner."

It was around four in the afternoon when Rick came up to the office to inform me that he was leaving for the day, the kitchen was clean, and the food was stored. He removed the apron when he entered the office, letting it hang from his fingers. The sight of the apron dangling in front of me sparked a memory in the back of my mind.

Gazing at me with his disturbingly blue-violet eyes, Rick decided to tell me I looked tired. I thanked him for the compliment and like most smart men, he realized he'd committed an innocent but treacherous faux pas and duly headed for the office door. I asked him to leave the apron behind. Rick was finished with the cleanup and probably wanted to get home to take a shower. Kitchen grease has a way of attaching itself to your skin; the lingering smell becomes a sour taste in your mouth.

I recognized the heavy-duty apron and realized it was Daniel's. I borrowed it once to scrape sticky residue off the bathroom wall. I'd hated to think what it might be, and, using a sharp blade, poked a hole in it by mistake. Daniel wasn't upset and we patched it with glue. It was a small puncture and no one else would have noticed, but I knew where to look.

Daniel kept it in the kitchen, hanging beside the stove. He relied on it regularly. It proved to be invaluable protection when working with toxic grease removers. The acid-based chemicals he used had to be powerful enough to clean the oven walls coated with carbon as hard as a diamonds.

Tony's butchers wore them, too. I recalled shuddering the first time I walked into the cutting room at Superior Meats. I'd had a special order for a small party and the chef had ordered me to pick up twenty pieces of oxtail precisely the same weight and size. If you have ever seen a whole oxtail you know that, like most tails, they start off wide at one end and narrow to a point at the other. Consequently, there are a lot of odd sizes. The butcher asked me to come inside to the cutting room to choose the tail size I needed. I had never been beyond the sacred corded rope that separated the public area from the private.

Fluorescent light bounced off the enameled tiled walls. The white room was immaculate, a surreal environment of glistening stainless steel with tell-tale nests of sawdust in the corners. The piercing screams from metal hitting bone forced me to cover my ears. The men stopped sawing and turned to watch me. I was out of my depth and they knew it, all sly smiles and winks behind my back.

Safety regulations made it mandatory for the butchers to wear the aprons in the cutting room. A heavy rubber surface applied to a thick woven backing made the protective garment impregnable to blood and burns. Covering the upper chest area to the underarms, the apron hung below the knees almost to the ankles, a chain-mail vest underneath it prevented flying bones and blades from maiming them. Still, I was pretty certain there wasn't one amongst them who wasn't missing digit or two. Two of the younger men who were operating industrial grinders removed yellow Plexiglas goggles, letting them dangle around their necks. Neither one of them allowed a *soupçon* of decency or self-consciousness to stop them from looking me over from top to bottom. I felt nude and trussed, ready to be flipped onto a table. Screw the oxtails. I got out of there fast.

Still at my desk, I went online and moved funds out of my personal line of credit to pay last week's wages. The creditors and feds would have to form a line. It's not like we've never been forced to close before. I should have some kind of financial protection in place by now, but I don't.

Last year, an underground main water valve broke, bursting through the foundation's ancient limestone. The foaming water flooded the basement in seconds. If anyone had been in the staff changing room or in the washroom, they would have drowned. Fortunately, it was midnight and the only one left was Abdul, the dishwasher. He was about to leave through the back door when he heard a strange gurgling sound in the stairwell. Nervously, he grabbed the chef's flashlight off the salamander and thrust the light at the sound. I heard the shock was so great he nearly fell in. Instead of stairs, he saw a black well of rising water lapping at his runners.

He went running down to the fire station around the corner. By the time they arrived in their trucks, the water was spilling out through the doors and cascading in rivers along the gutters. The firemen closed off the area and cleared the building, making sure no one was left inside. The emergency hydro task force was called in to disconnect the hydro lines with massive steel cutters. Although I was already half asleep in bed, Rick gave me a blow-by-blow account of the ordeal from his cellphone. Another reason I don't like phones.

A year before the great flood, gunshot spray from a drug-bust-turned-street-chase blew out an entire section of the dining-room wall. Good thing it was after midnight. Rick had just ushered the last couple out the front door. Shutting off the main control switch for the restaurant's lights, he left by the side door, stepping out into the cool night air. No sooner had he zipped up his jacket when he heard the bullets ripping through the restaurant behind the closed door.

The repairs to the interior slowed us down for a few days and the patched wall is still noticeable to this day. It's proudly pointed out by our waiters hoping to impress tourists with Toronto's dangerous city nightlife. I've been trying to curb them of this annoying habit. Too many of our employees from the encompassing rural townships are preoccupied with the search for lurid excitement.

I'm happy to close for Hollywood anytime. They pay good money. *Fabulous* money and I get to see a few stars. Many movies have been shot in Walker's Way because it resembles a New York–style restaurant. Many years ago, soon after I opened for business, a major American film company used the restaurant for an action movie starring Billy Dee Williams. They set off mini-explosions in a violent re-enactment that ironically blew out the same wall that would be shot up years later.

Unfortunately, no amount of policy insurance covers possible food poisoning or health closures. In the face of bankruptcy, I've always clung to the illusion that at least I eat and drink for free. I'm not fond of dining out, anyway. To me it's a busman's holiday. I just can't relax. I either want to correct the spelling on the specials menu or tell the waiter to turn the music down.

After kiting a few checks and making a few more pledges of payment to a list of hopeful creditors, I stared at the transom of stained glass adorning the bay window. Daniel's story didn't add up. I really couldn't be sure that the voice I heard in the hall (at the exhibition before I got my head conked) was Daniel's. More and more, I couldn't justify his actions for walking out on me and running home to his sister. I tried to make a connection to the mystery voice in the convention hall, but all I could remember was someone not wanting to be part of the grand scheme. If it was Daniel, who was he talking to?

All alone in the office, the sounds of life and cooking smells drifting down from the apartment above taunted me. Rick was on his way home, eager to prepare dinner for his recent fling. I was envious imagining the exotic delicacies marinating in his fridge and the spectacular year of Chablis he no doubt had waiting to be chilled. Rick was smart, very funny, knew how to cook, and was irresistibly charming. When he needed a new girlfriend, all he had to do was open a window and yell, "Next!"

chapter eight

I decided to go home and make dinner for my son. I'm not a great cook, but I've watched the chefs over the years and a few memorable dishes have stuck in my head. Jon was a vegetarian and loved my pasta prima vera. Personally I find it lacks something. I'm guessing the meat. I'd rather have a gooey grilled-cheese sandwich with bacon any day. I loved Scotch, wine, and beer in that order. Oh, and sugar, I mustn't forget sugar. I could feel a heart attack coming on just thinking about it. I'd be a lot fatter or even dead if I didn't visit the gym three times a week. My mother said my metabolism will change and I better be careful about gaining weight that I can't shed when I'm older. She's hilarious.

After talking about my situation ad nauseam, Jon suggested I talk to the people in the market personally. See what they know, do a little digging. I agreed. Tomorrow the locals and I would have a little chit-chat.

The young female cop who drove me home after my hospital visit called at the house just after dinner. Jon said he was meeting her for a drink at the pub on the corner. I thought they would make a cute couple. Seems they got together while I was on the east coast, and, speaking of couples, I wondered what the whimsical Winn was doing. Hopefully, he was making some headway into uncovering the truth about the two murders, a sleazy butcher, and an underhanded councillor. Were their deaths connected and how was my chef involved?

I had no money coming in and almost no line of credit left. I would have to tighten my belt until this mess was cleared up. The word "bankrupt" was right on the tip of my tongue when I noticed a car's engine was idling out front of the house. I looked out my bedroom window to see an unmarked police car parked at the curb. Detective Winn got out. The doorbell rang.

I ran to the hall mirror and discovered I was due for a serious makeover. My dirty sweatpants sagged heavily in the back, suggesting I was carrying a fresh load, and a pair of Jon's size-twelve tube socks worn around the house as slippers were about as sexy as clown shoes. My face had been scrubbed clean of makeup and my hair brushed one hundred times with my head bent over my knees. I tried to pat it back into shape, but the static made it stick to my hand.

The doorbell rang again. After nearly tripping down the stairs in the giant socks, I pulled open the door and greeted him. "Hi, Detective, fancy meeting you here." I waved cheerfully with one hand while trying to get my hair under control with the other.

"Hello, Ms. Walker, I hope you don't mind me dropping in unannounced. I have a couple of questions I was hoping to ask …" He paused, looking at my hair. "I don't want to intrude. If you're busy, I can make it another time."

"No, of course not, I'm just doing the laundry. No clean clothes left, that's why I'm dressed like this." A bold-faced lie.

"But, still ..." He left the words hanging.

"Please, detective, come in. I'll put the kettle on, unless you prefer something stronger."

"Coffee is fine with me, thanks." He followed me into the kitchen.

I put the kettle on and said, "I'll be right back." I ran upstairs, changed into my black jeans, threw off the sweatshirt, and pulled on a tight clean T-shirt. I flew back down the stairs leaned my chin on my hand and asked coyly, "Tell me, what brings you out here? Am I one of your suspects, too?"

He did a double-take, hesitated, and then replied, "I was on my way home. And no, you're not a suspect. Maybe I should be treating you as one, except your alibi checks out." He turned a wooden kitchen chair about face, and straddling the seat, sat down. He folded his arms across the top of the chair back and leaned his head on his arms. It made him seem younger and more vulnerable.

"You never asked me for an alibi," I pointed out.

"My rookie, Susan Waltham, the same one who drove you home and is rapidly becoming your son's new friend, filed a report." He removed the little notebook from his jacket and tapped it. I placed two cups of instant on the table.

"Says here that you were both at a Raptors game. We know it went into overtime and didn't get out until midnight. Mr. Vieira was dead by then. We also know you took a cab home with your son, we checked that out, too."

I bristled. "So she was using my boy to get information when all the while he thought she liked him."

"She does like him. It was an innocent discovery. The night they went out, Jon reached into his pocket to pay for a jug of beer and two ticket stubs from the game fell out. She followed it up with a few questions and made a note of it for me. Look, she's a cop, what can I say?" He looked at me and blinked. "Somehow you don't look like a basketball fan to me."

"It's quality time with my adult kid and I'll take it any way I can. What about you, do you have children?"

"No, my wife and I never got around to it. Instead I got a house and mortgage payments to keep me company. She moved directly out of our house and into another guy's. I guess we'll sort the mess out with the house during the divorce."

I had to ask. "Wow, she moved right in with another guy? You didn't see it coming?"

"I wasn't home much. I used work as an excuse to stay away. We weren't happy."

There was a long drawn-out pause and he asked me, "Do you regret not being married anymore?"

"The only thing I regret is those sweatpants."

"No comment." He chuckled.

Well, weren't we having fun? I smiled and asked, "You said you were on your way home. Do you live around here?

"About a half a mile down the road." He took a sip of the coffee and grimaced. "Instant?"

"Sorry, I keep forgetting to pick up groceries for the house. Shopping all the time for the business leaves me tired and my own cupboards bare."

"Instant is fine. I'm a little surprised, that's all, you owning a fancy restaurant and everything. Believe me I'm not complaining."

I got the feeling he was and wished I had something better to offer. Why was I so sensitive around this man? Maybe it was a reaction to his unorthodox method of police sleuthing: rogue interrogation mixed with romantic undertones.

"How did it go with Daniel? I know I'm not supposed to ask, but he is my chef and I honestly think he's innocent. I would like to get him back to work as soon as possible."

"We're not holding Daniel. I questioned him for the better part of the afternoon after he arrived from Halifax with his sister. She waited outside the interview room for him. I get the impression she's the brains in the family. A lawyer is probably waiting in the wings by now and I didn't want to get bogged down with a legal entanglement. I let him go, this time with a serious warning not to leave town again. I need more information, more time."

"Tell me the truth, Detective. What do you really think about Daniel?"

"Other than your young chef's unfortunate involvement with Anthony Vieira, I believe Daniel doesn't have any knowledge of either of the two deaths. I don't believe he was having an affair with Maria, or you for that matter, and I apologize for the presumption. It seems ridiculous now."

I resented the ridiculous part, but sighed and blew a thin whistle through my teeth. "Whew. That's a relief."

"Your chef stated that Tony Vieira, besides causing a severe case of food poisoning, was also going to spread rumours the new spring cattle show was plagued with mad cow disease. Why would he do that?"

"I suppose he felt that a simple case of food poisoning wouldn't be enough to cause a scandal. I mean people experience mild cases all the time, and since most of the symptoms are similar to the flu it's generally not reported. I've never heard of anyone trying to intentionally cause food poisoning. It's a pretty unreliable means of payback, if you know what I mean. Only in a few isolated cases where the person's immune system is weakened would a severe reaction be fatal. The elderly and the young are more susceptible, for sure." As soon as I said that, I remembered the old guy wheeled out of the restaurant. The hairs on my neck stood up and a shiver ran down my spine.

"BSE stands for mad cow disease. I know what the first two letters stand for, but for the life of me I can't remember what the E stands for."

"It stands for *Encelopathy. Bovine spongiform encelopathy* is a controversial subject. It's a disease no one wants to be connected with, especially cattle ranchers and dairy farmers. A fabricated lie linking the disease to the show would tarnish the show's image and threaten the livelihood of the demonstrators and the only proven method of detecting it is through autopsy of the suspected animals. There would be a lynch mob from here to Calgary looking for Albright."

"Okay, I can see why the councillor might have had a motive for killing Tony, but he's dead. And I understand Tony would have killed Albright, but he's dead, too. If we maintain Daniel was incapable of murder, then who killed them?"

"How about his wife?"

"She has an alibi. Besides she was almost killed herself, along with the councillor."

Our conversation was rolling along nicely and I thought we were really getting the hang of this when the metaphorical shoe dropped.

"I'm wondering if you could do me a favor. It would help me in my investigation."

"Yes…?"

"I like Maria."

Well, stick a fork in and tell me when I'm done. I knew it. I knew he wasn't interested in me. He's been pretending all along. "She is lovely," I spit out.

He screwed up his eyes. "Not *like*, as in I'm attracted to her. It's a police term. Don't you watch television? I *like* her for a possible connection in this case."

There must be something wrong with me. I turned my back and wiped the counter so he couldn't see the relief on my face.

He continued, "I think there's more to her than there appears on the surface. She's keeping something bottled up inside. Something's bothering her and she's worried sick I'll find out what it is."

I faced him again. "You interviewed her. You said she was in shock after her discovery of Mr. Tony's body. Maybe that's all it was."

"She was in shock initially and then when she came to the station for questioning, she had changed."

"How do you mean *changed?*"

"I've seen enough court-room attire in my life to recognize a futile attempt to appear in control. She had on a black two-piece suit, stockings, and low-heeled pumps. Her hair was pulled straight back and she wasn't wearing make-up. I admit it was difficult concentrating on the interview because the plain Jane routine only heightened her beauty. I had even more trouble deciphering her mood. Corpses down in the morgue show more expression."

"What do you want me to do?"

"Listen, it's probably just me being a cop. I'm trying to cover all the bases. Forget I asked."

"No, what is it?"

"I thought if you saw her in the market again you could talk to her, see if she opens up."

"Why would she do that? I told you that we're not friends."

"And I believe you, but sometimes people open up to strangers. Especially if they want to get something off their chest."

Winn looked at the on the kitchen stove clock. "I just realized that the time on the stove hasn't changed since I got here. It says 9:10. According to my watch, it's a lot later than that."

"It's been the same time for over two years. I haven't got around to changing the fuse. Don't feel badly, it fools a lot of people. And hey, it's right twice a day!"

The detective stood up, arched his back, and removed his jacket from the back of the chair.

"Before you leave, tell me what it is I'm supposed to be looking for?" I asked.

"When we questioned the Superior Meat employees about working for Mr. Vieira, they all said it was a nice place to work, no complaints, and no comments about their jobs. But the answers were too pat. And when the questions were regarding Maria, they said they didn't know anything and got all shifty."

"What did they mean by *anything?*"

"That's what I wanted to know. We did a personal background check on each of them and found out that one of the girls had an invalid social insurance card with a bogus number. She had only been in the country for two months. No visa, just here on a visitor's pass. We threatened her with detention if she didn't divulge how she obtained it and eventually she cracked. She said she borrowed it from Maria."

"Was it Maria's?"

"No. And when we asked Maria if she gave it to her, she said the girl was lying to prevent being sent back home. No way of proving any of it right now. We're bringing in the Immigration Bureau to investigate and it's not my problem to solve. I've got two murders and if they're connected in any way we'll know soon enough." Winn stretched his back again and looked down at his watch. "Right, I should be heading home. I've got an early court appearance tomorrow." I walked him to the door, spiralling quickly into a grumpy mood and he sensed it.

"It's not unusual for the police to ask for help in an investigation, you know. I'm not trying to use or manipulate you in any way and I don't want you to do anything you shouldn't. Keep your eyes and ears open and trust your instincts. You want everything to return to normal as soon as possible, so help me. I know you're smart. And maybe someone in the market might talk to you because they like you. They sure as hell don't like me."

"I'll think about it, Detective. Drive carefully."

Winn bent over and kissed me on the cheek, "It was nice talking to you, thank you for the coffee."

I washed the cups and rinsed out the teapot. The kiss worried me. I was a dyed-in-the-wool cynic and my mind was racing. I needed a diversion, but having forgotten to visit the library on the way home, I had nothing to read. I climbed into bed and began to compile a grocery list for tomorrow. Starting with ground coffee, I instantly nodded off.

chapter nine

The sky was heavily overcast and the clouds promised a day of rain. Lying on my side I watched shades of watery light play listlessly on the bedroom floor. Reflecting on my state of affairs, I wondered what I'd do if I didn't own a restaurant. There were other businesses just as financially challenging, for example, art galleries and bookstores, but then where would I eat?

I shuffled down to the kitchen and remembered my oath to follow a better diet. After forcing down a guilt-induced breakfast of hemp granola and gagging on the thick pulpy residue of organic orange juice, I drove downtown to the market and parked in my usual spot in front of the Contraroses' vegetable store. The street was open to traffic again and the security tape had been removed. Eddie scared me half to death by coming around behind the car and rapping loudly on my window.

"I don't have nothin' to put in the car today," he shouted, his face pressed against the glass.

I rolled down the window and blasted Eddie for sneaking up on me. Holding my hand over my heart, I asked if he was trying to kill me. Eddie looked terrified. I told him I was kidding around. I could be a real jerk sometimes and told him that, too. My apology worked like magic. He ran ahead, diving around vegetable bins stored under a sagging awning, hollering and waving for me to follow him inside.

It had been pouring rain since I got out of bed and the store's faded red-and-green striped canvas threatened to dump a bucket of water onto my head. I raced into the store, hard on his heels, when abruptly he turned around and stopped. I ran straight into his arms. He lifted me a foot off the ground in a bear hug and then, releasing me just as quickly, disappeared through a trap door to the fruit cellar below.

Getting additional information about Mr. Tony's death from Louis, Eddie's grandfather, proved to be futile, however. He didn't want to talk ill of the dead and crossed himself judiciously when I mentioned his name. A tangible mood of depression lingered in the damp market air, and with Superior Meats closed, business was slower than usual. The meat store was popular city-wide and drew a number of potential customers to the neighbouring establishments. Another empty building on the street looked bad. Besides a few curiosity-seekers, the market was dead.

Louise's cheese store was closed. I looked in the window through the sun-protected, yellow-cellophane-covered glass and saw a notice tacked to the register at the front. A community meeting was being held in St. Timothy's church around the corner on Spadina Avenue. Mrs. Wong came down the sidewalk toward me. We exchanged a few rounds of conversational Cantonese, phrases she had been patiently teaching me for years, and then I asked, in English, if she was going to the meeting.

Not only was she going to the meeting, but all the storekeepers were attending. Very important meeting, she stressed. With the former city representative dead and his underling in charge, the meeting would be important to their future. I asked her if I could come. She said I could be her friend. I assumed she meant guest and agreed to meet her at her dry goods store at 6:30 later that day. We would walk over together.

In the meantime, the customer who caused my restaurant to be closed down should be paid a visit. Although he didn't ask to get sick, I wasn't feeling very sympathetic toward the man. He was recuperating at St. Mike's and when Rick called the hospital in the morning to enquire about his progress, a nurse told him Mr. Randolph's quarantine was lifted.

"Was he seeing visitors now?" he asked.

"Oh yes," she said merrily. "He was feeling much better." Rick volunteered to go, but I said I'd probably better. Good public relations to have the owner of famed "death's door" eatery personally visit a happily recovering customer.

I picked up a bouquet of overpriced, albeit fragrant, miniature white roses in the hospital gift shop and consulted the directory before heading up to the ninth floor. Mr. Randolph was sitting up in bed eating lemon jelly and looking grim. This wasn't going to be easy.

"Hello, Mr. Randolph. My name is Liz Walker, mind if I come in?" I said with my biggest smile ever.

"I never mind talking to a pretty girl," he answered, surprising me with an equally big smile.

"You might change your mind. I have to be honest with you; I'm the owner of the restaurant where you got sick."

He put the jelly down on the night table. "Have they told you?" he asked me sternly.

Okay, I thought, *here we go*. This is where he's

going to tell me how much he's suing the restaurant for. I wished Rick had come instead.

"I'm very, very sorry you got food poisoning at the restaurant, Mr. Randolph. We don't know how it happened. I shop for everything fresh and we take extreme precautions when handling food. We have all the coloured boards for cleaning and preparing foods. I mean we have red for raw meat and yellow for fish and green for produce. We have sanitation units at all the food stations and I, I ..."

"Please stop, Mrs. Walker. I have something to tell you." He held up a hand, halting my babbling soliloquy.

"Call me Liz." I was trying to be friendly.

"My wife is sick, too."

"What?" I gasped. "She wasn't at the restaurant, was she? I thought you were alone. Somebody must have got it wrong." I would kill Rick for not telling me.

"Nope," he said, "my wife got sick at home after eating a chicken sandwich. The same chicken I made my sandwich from the day before. She was out of town at an old girlfriend's the day I went to your restaurant for dinner. Never been a big fan of cooking for myself, not very New Age, I'm afraid, and I've been to your place a few times and liked the food. Anyway, now she's sick. After that power failure we had from the storm last week she forgot to throw out the mayonnaise. She only buys the whole egg kind and it had turned ripe with salmonella." He drew in a breath and suddenly looked a hundred years old. A thin wisp of gray hair fell limp across his cheek; a puff of air from his curled lips removed it.

"She's down the hall in room 9E if you want to say hello," he suggested shyly.

It was my turn to be angry, except I felt for the guy. I didn't say a word.

"I'm so sorry, my wife is, too. If your business has suffered in any way, I feel responsible. I would be willing to call the newspaper and tell them it had nothing to do with your restaurant. The hospital is contacting the health board to allow you to open again as soon as possible."

He seemed sincerely upset and he wasn't solely to blame for causing the restaurant's unfortunate closure. My chef was mysteriously linked to the slaying of Anthony Vieira and the fatal poisoning of a notable public city official. The sequence of events after Mr. Tony was found butchered would lead everyone to the conclusion that we were just as likely to be responsible for the food poisoning of one of our customers. "Something fishy going on there, better stay away, they would say to each other," nodding their heads in agreement. I gave Mr. Randolph a kiss on his smelly forehead and sent his wife my blessings for a speedy recovery.

I was so excited that the restaurant was going to reopen I couldn't wait to leave the hospital and return to work. First I needed to phone Rick to tell him to notify the staff. Having left my cell in the car, I asked an orderly outside the door if there was a public phone on the floor and he pointed to the end of the hall.

Halfway down the hall, Maria D'Agnole from the butcher shop ran straight into me. She was crying so hard, she didn't recognize me. When I asked her if she needed help she shook her head and practically jumped in the elevator when the door slid open. Obviously she had just received some bad news. I hoped it wasn't her father. The girls at Mr. Tony's were talking about his health one day and I listened in. I think some days I was invisible to them, just a number holder waiting for my order to be filled. I heard a lot of stuff that way.

I headed for the phones and looked into the patient's room from which Maria had fled. I expected to see her father, Mr. D'Agnole, lying in the bed with a heart monitor beeping faintly, not a beautiful golden-haired woman, around thirty, lounging on top of the bedcovers.

Instead of the prescribed hospital garb, she had on a hot pink peignoir set, which offset her tawny skin. A food show, on the tiny television suspended at the end of her bed, held her complete attention.

The patient's names were displayed in large print on dry-erase board outside all the rooms and Mrs. Cecilia Vieira was the only name on the board. I saw this woman once before in Superior Meats and assumed she was one of the store's young recruits who were constantly passing through. I knocked lightly on the doorframe before entering a few steps into the room. She turned and poised with a chocolate halfway to her mouth, gave me the once-over from top to bottom. Was it just me or did everyone who ever worked at Mr. Tony's learn how to give the evil eye? I twitched involuntarily.

"Hello, Mrs. Vieira. I was just visiting another patient on this floor and I recognized your name on the board." Lamely I pointed to the door with a silly half-grin. If this woman didn't stop glaring at me soon, I was going to leave by backing up step by step until I was in the elevator. She had one powerful mojo going on and I didn't want to get hexed in the back when I tore out of there. Then she smiled. Time stood still. Instead of being repelled, I felt the tractor beam pull of her eyes pull me into the room.

"Don't mind me, honey. I was trying to remember where I've seen you before. Now I know. You used to come into the store to shop. You own that cute little restaurant down on Queen Street, don't you?" Her voice was cigarette-husky. It took me a second before I could answer,

"Yes, that's my restaurant. It's called Walker's Way. I hope I'm not disturbing you. I wanted to offer my condolences. I'm very sorry for your loss."

"Don't be. My husband won't be missed, not by me, anyway. I'm free at last and once the will is read next week I'll be rich, too. I get all his property and I can do anything I want with it."

"I'm sure that's some consolation, but you must be very frightened. First someone takes his life and then you and Stephen Albright are poisoned. I'm sorry to hear about the councillor. I didn't know him, but I take it the two of you were close. Sounds like someone might be targeting you."

She popped the chocolate into her mouth and chose another from a two-layered box sitting on her lap. Were the chocolates gifts from friendly well-wishers, or perhaps a secret admirer? I wanted to ask her about her affair with the late Stephen Albright, but was too much of a chicken and felt I had already said enough. I didn't want to get eyeballed again. Swiftly she thrust the candy at me, and, pointing under the bed, said, "Help yourself, I've got lots. There are two more boxes, down there somewhere."

I bent over to take a look and straightened. What was I doing? Who cared if she had a stash of chocolates under the bed? Between her vivid good looks and the sultry voice, the woman was a calculated distraction. Not many men would be able to resist her sexuality. I took a candy to be polite and joined her in watching a show demonstrating the fine art of fondue cooking. After twenty seconds of mind-numbing film footage, I thought, *fondue this*, and made a private gesture at the television set.

Then I asked Mrs. Vieira, "I ran into Maria D'Agnole in the hall a few minutes ago. She seemed terribly upset. I thought maybe she had been visiting you and wondered if she was all right? I know her father has been ill."

"Listen, sweetie, I didn't even know she had a father. I told her that now that Tony's gone she shouldn't expect any more cash for her favours. She was his whore — as if the world didn't know — and the fun was over."

That was harsh. Maria never looked like she was having fun to me. More likely, she had been playing up to Tony because she wanted to keep her job. I took a chance and said to her outright, "Seems like everyone who knew your husband is under suspicion. My chef is being treated as their prime suspect. I've been questioned and I know the Superior Meats employees have been interviewed. Of course the residents of the market are very upset with this investigation hanging over their heads. I guess I don't have to tell you about that, do I? I mean, the wife is usually the first person they accuse."

"Yeah, well, they're not, and I shouldn't be discussing this with you in any case."

"Why not?"

"Because the police warned me not to talk to anyone and I don't know you from Adam."

Our conservation was ending on a low note. Mrs. Vieira's smile had vanished, and, not wanting to cause her any painful memories or invoke a curse, I wished her well and left. I noticed the same orderly who gave me directions to the phone was standing outside the door again.

"Find the phone alright ma'am?"

I nodded and smiled. I get called "ma'am" one more time today and I'll scream.

My new priority was getting the restaurant open. My existence depended on it, not to mention my staff's. We all have loans to keep up, bank loans, car loans, student loans, shark loans, all of the above. My engines were revving.

I beetled it through the main lobby of the hospital, agilely side-stepping patients dragging drip poles, solemn-faced nurses, and lost visitors with flowering plants in their hands. I saw the sign for the cafeteria and knowing Walker's was closed, thought a nice cup of tea and a cinnamon Danish might hit the spot. I made a hard right toward the pastry cart.

Maria D'Agnole was sitting at a table in the far corner. I put a teabag in a Styrofoam cup, filled it with boiling water from a spigot attached to an enormous copper drum kettle, and paid for it. I forgot about the bun.

"Hi, Maria. Mind if I join you?"

"Hi, um, I'm sorry, I forget your name. Please sit down."

"Liz Walker, I used to come into the meat store a lot."

"Oh, yes, I knew I recognized you. I talked to you a couple of times in the market bakery. Please excuse me, I'm a little distracted."

"Is it your father, will he be all right?"

She looked confused and slightly vacant, like she was mulling something over.

"I'm sorry if I seem nosy," I said. "It's just that I lost my father this year and you look upset. If you need to talk about it, I can lend you an ear."

"Thanks, but it's not just that. You heard about my boss Mr. Tony being killed? It's been a terrible shock for me. I understand that your chef is the murder suspect."

"He was, maybe he still is, but the police haven't arrested him. Not enough evidence or motive, apparently. Were you close to Mr. Tony?"

Maria bristled at the suggestion. "Where would you get an idea like that?"

"You just said you were in shock and it's not hard to see you've been crying."

"I'm not made of stone. I found his body, you know. I'll never get that picture out of my mind. It's all starting to sink in. How do you think I'd react?"

"Sorry, I thought you were good friends."

"I despised the man. He was repugnant." She was venomous and in full attack mode.

"Are you surprised that I would use such a word? I graduated from high school with honours and I'm taking a correspondence course through the University of Toronto to further my studies."

This was a side of Maria I had never seen before. I didn't know why I ever felt sorry for her. She certainly wasn't the poor little immigrant girl I had first taken her for. Remembering Winn's request, I ignored the bitterness in her voice and pretended concern.

"You were fairly young when you first started the job at Superior Meats, weren't you?"

"I wasn't the only one. There were other girls my age."

"You've been there quite a while? You must have liked working for him at one time."

She settled down, gaining control quickly. "It was difficult at first. Most of the girls quit because of the long hours and low wages. I didn't have the luxury, I'm afraid. A few of the older women had butcher's degrees from schools they attended in the old country, but they were of little use at Superior. The store had a strict policy — men only were allowed in the cutting room."

Maria shuddered. I wondered what she was thinking.

I asked her quietly, "What is it, Maria?"

"In the beginning, when I undersold or wasn't fast enough, I was sent back to the packing station where the large commercial orders were made up for delivery. I hated that windowless room, so claustrophobic and always bone cold. It was like being buried alive."

"Things will be a lot different at the store now, I would think."

Maria smiled, "Oh, I think so, I'm quite looking forward to it."

After my conversation with the widow upstairs, I hoped she had alternative means of employment.

"I dropped in to say hello to your boss's wife," I said. "She seemed fine. I mean being poisoned doesn't seem to have bothered her much. In fact she seemed in a pretty good mood."

Maria's eyes became instantly hooded and she looked down at her watch. Obviously she didn't want to talk about it any further. She twisted her watch around on her wrist so that she could read it. "I'm sorry, I really have to run. Since the store is closed today, I booked a dance rehearsal for this afternoon and I don't want to be late." She stood, spilling a little unfinished tea in her cup on the table. "Nice talking to you. Bye." She left quickly.

I was sliding my chair back and reaching for my purse when I spied a gold plastic shoe bag under the table. I opened it and pulled out a small piece of silky material. Several flyers were wrapped around it and a deck of playing cards still in their box spilled out and fell to the floor. I was about to pick up the cards, but Maria beat me to it. She palmed the deck of cards in one hand and reached her other hand out to me. "That's mine. It's my dance costume." I handed everything over to her except for one of the flyers. I read the bold black lettering printed across the red paper:

TOSCANO'S DANCE HALL
DANCE COMPETITION

FIRST PRIZE $5000.00 DOLLARS
REOPENING CELEBRATION
JOIN US FOR FOOD, FUN AND
DANCE, DANCE, DANCE

DOOR CHARGE: $25.00 PER PERSON,
COUPLES $40.00

"Do you dance competitively?" I inquired.

She smiled wide. Nice teeth. "Yes, my boyfriend, Nicky, and I are contestants. We qualified for the finals last night. When we win this competition we'll qualify for other national contests. I'm so excited. I've always wanted to travel."

Finally, something she was happy to talk about.

"I'm selling tickets to help out with the door, would you like one?" Maria asked.

"Sure, why not. What kind of dancing?"

"It's all Latin, rumba, tango, salsa, you know. We don't do any ballroom style."

"Sounds wonderful, I love the tango. I'll take two." I figured I could find someone to go with me, maybe Jon or Rick, although they probably had dates. Well, maybe one of my old girlfriends. I haven't seen Diana for a while. Then a plan occurred to me. If my new detective friend wanted more information on Maria, then he might be interested in accompanying me to the dance. I threw my head back and let out a triumphant laugh, it was genius, I tell you, pure genius.

chapter ten

Rick was on his way to Walker's. The chief health inspector had notified him that the source of food poisoning was not attributed to Walker's, a fact that Mr. Randolph already confessed to me in the hospital. The sanction was lifted. However, we would have to wait for an official green pass to put in the window before we could legally reopen. Our local inspector phoned to say he wasn't sure what time he could meet Rick to give him one. In any case, Rick wanted to wait for him at the restaurant and would call me as soon as he heard any news.

Whether we opened tonight or the next morning, the staff had to be alerted and the prep started from scratch. Rick was anxious to get the show on the road. In the meantime, I had somewhere else I wanted to go. It was almost 4:30, hours before I promised to meet Mrs. Wong for the market community meeting later tonight. I had plenty of time to spare.

Unable to get my Danish in the hospital's food court and feeling peckish, I drove east along Front Street to the St. Lawrence indoor market. A cavernous building open from the ground floor to the vaulted, sky-lighted ceiling above, it was large enough to hold a plane inside its belly. Hundreds of vendor stalls and cafés crowded the floor instead.

At the bottom of a sweep of terrazzo stairs, hidden in one of the corners of the basement, behind a massive, supporting stone pillar, and next to the men's washroom, an elderly Dutch lady wearing authentic wooden shoes sold me an aluminum pie plate brimming with cheesy garlic perogies. I am the private eye of food, if it's good, I will find it.

I took my stash to my car parked outside the Old Spaghetti Factory and ate them while watching the nine-to-fivers leave work for the day. I used a half a box of Kleenex to wipe the dripping oil from my face (to my dismay, the supply of wet towels I kept in the glove box had run out). By the time I finished cleaning myself up, it was time to head back.

Rick still hadn't called, making me apprehensive about our reopening tonight. Rick was one of those people who liked to keep the channels of communication open at all times. I called him at the restaurant, but there was no answer and no response in the office. I drove home and changed into heavier clothes. The weather was a lot colder than when I left the house this morning.

I met Mrs. Wong in front of her fruit store at a 6:00 p.m., meticulously locking the old wooden door with bolts and chains. Citing numerous break-ins amongst the area vendors this year, she was considering the installation of a metal security gate across the front entrance. We walked around the corner to St. Timothy's church through a light rain, not hard enough for me to want to be burdened with an awkward umbrella.

The meeting was held in the church's basement Sunday-school room. I recognized a few familiar faces from the meat store, sales girls who had waited on me over the years. We smiled at each other. None of us had exchanged phone numbers or even first names, but we shared common information about each other: whose husband shovelled the snow, whose kids were in what colleges, and where vacations were spent. The girls knew I owned a restaurant, but I doubted any one of them could tell you its location.

Maria was sitting in the front row beside Louise Kozinski, owner of the Cheese Emporium, and when I tried to catch her eye, she pretended to be engaged in a riveting conversation. She was obviously avoiding me and then it dawned on me. She hadn't mentioned the community meeting when I saw her at the hospital. Was she suddenly embarrassed about not inviting me, or was she afraid to acknowledge our acquaintance in front of the others?

The Superior Meats sales girls and a several butchers took up the remainder of the seats along the first row. I wondered if the girl with the false working permit was there, too, or was she in police detention awaiting a boat trip to take her back home? Eddie and Louis sat in the second row with fellow produce sellers, including Joseph Hamilton, who supplied the best plantain outside of Jamaica. Eddie waved to me gleefully and his grandfather nodded solemnly.

Mrs. Wong answered my question about the two German brothers, Hans and Karl Jorgen, the bakers. According to her, the brothers still lived over the sixty-year-old bakery their father started when he immigrated here after the Second World War. The market was predominantly Jewish at that time and Karl senior, their father, had found it hard fitting in. His kindly old neighbour, Mr. Solomon, felt sorry for the young immigrant with a family to feed and suggested he make steamed bagels and flatbreads.

Mr. Solomon went so far as to give Karl his mother's treasured Hebrew recipe bequeathed to him and kept under lock and key in her documents box. Mr. Solomon was long gone now and so was Mr. Jorgen, but his two sons continued to get up at 4:00 a.m. every morning to bake the delicious Montreal bagels, flatbread, and poppy-seed cakes that were famous city-wide. The two brothers, their wives, and six noisy children took up an entire row.

A few of the seats remained empty on both sides of the fish-store owners, reeking of — you guessed it — fish, and a group of nattily dressed second-hand clothiers filled the rest of the seats. The trendy new and used clothing stores were spreading steadily, replacing the overly populated vegetable stands. I loved wearing vintage dresses when I was younger. I'd look like a bag lady if I wore one now.

Mrs. Wong and I sat in the back row. I didn't want to stick out and she had to leave early to cook for her family. She counted on her fingers out loud to me: a husband, her mother and father, his mother and father, two sons, two daughters, her sister, her sister's husband, and their infant baby. I find it hard cooking for two. Just because I own a restaurant doesn't mean I like to cook.

Louise stood and walked purposely to the fold-out banquet table at the front of the room. She asked if she could get started with the meeting and everyone settled down.

"First, I want to thank all of you for attending tonight's meeting. I realize it's not a nice night out and many of you would like to go home. Again, thank you for coming. Some of you are full-time residents and some of you own businesses in the area. Many of you are employed by the local businesses, as well." She nodded at the girls in the front row. "Nevertheless, we all have the same agenda tonight. It is very important that we welcome Mr. Tilson; our new representative from City Hall. We are a community that needs to speak out and be heard. As Mr. Albright's assistant for the last few years, Mr. Tilson has become familiar with some of our more serious concerns. Crime on the street has risen. Drugs and drug users have become more noticeable, even during daytime hours. Garbage litters the streets and stores sit vacant, inviting rats and other vermin. The future of the market depends on action. Hopefully, tonight our new representative will be able to answer your questions."

I was relieved that Louise didn't start the meeting with the words "my friends." Most likely the other residents of the market had deciphered her secret code by now.

"Albright pretended to listen to our problems and never did a ting. Full of excuses, him missing deadlines, and not enough names on our petitions." Joseph stood, half turning, to allow his question to reach the others. "Is Mr. Tilson going to be our new representative or is he just standing in temporarily because Albright is dead?"

Good question, I thought, and took note of the absence of "Mr." in front of Albright's name. He didn't warrant much sympathy from Joseph.

After looking toward the door and then at her watch, Louise offered an explanation: "Unfortunately, Joseph, since our new city councillor is not here, I can't answer that. I'm sure the traffic has held him up and he will be arriving momentarily. And I'm sure he means no disrespect. We all know how clogged the streets are at this time of day, especially with all this rain. Regardless, I think we should give Mr. Tilson a chance. Whether he's a permanent replacement or temporary doesn't matter. We need to get things done. The meeting tonight is about bringing the market back to life. Once we have made ourselves clear, city council will recognize our wishes and have no choice but to follow through on previous promises, regardless of any changes to the board."

"I haven't met the newcomer. What's he going to be like to work with?" asked Hans from his chair. He didn't have to stand. His voice was deep and resonant and I picked up on a slight northern European accent. "Mr. Albright was all talk and as Joseph pointed out, never did a *ting*." He and Joseph grinned at one another.

Louise answered, tight-lipped, "I understand Mr. Tilson is extremely supportive about this committee's objectives." Her face was becoming mottled with colour. She clearly wanted to move on to dealing with the new city representative. The fact that he hadn't showed yet wasn't being taken as a good omen. Tongues had begun to wag.

"So where is he?" asked Karl angrily.

Just when I thought Louise was going to pop a cork, the double doors to the church's meeting room burst opened and a young man bustled into the room. He was probably in his mid-thirties, still dealing with adult acne, and was pale and thin with a slightly concave chest.

"I apologize for my tardiness, Mrs. Kozinski," the man said nervously, obviously trying to ingratiate, and placed his rain-stained leather satchel on the table. Stepping in as area replacement, I thought he might be overwhelmed by his new station in life and a bit of a featherweight for the job. He reminded me of the type you see volunteering at voter's booths or going door to door for the Humane Society.

He slipped off a noticeably wet coat and glanced around for a suitable spot to let it dry. Not finding one and getting no help from Louise, he finally hung it over his chair. "Hello, everyone, my name is Arthur Tilson. Again, I apologize for being late. I was Mr. Albright's office assistant for three years and have assumed his position as councillor to the area. I'm sure all of you were just as shocked as I was to hear of his death and will miss him very much."

"If you were with him for so many years, how come you don't know we couldn't stand the son of a bitch?" asked a grocer whom I didn't recognize.

"Now let's watch what we say, Tomas, there are children in the room and I think we should forget about the past and focus on our future," said Louise patronizingly.

"Yes, yes absolutely," said Mr. Tilson, looking at his hands, which I could see shaking from my seat in the back, "that is precisely why I'm here, of course. Unfortunately the rain and traffic is not the sole reason why I am late. I went to the hospital to see Mrs. Cecilia Vieira."

"Mr. Tony's wife," whispered Mrs. Wong, in case I didn't know.

"She called me this morning and asked for a private meeting. She wished to personally inform me of her plans for the neighbourhood and since she is fully aware of this meeting, she thought it would be good for me to get this out on the table tonight."

Mr. Tilson cleared his throat like he had a canary stuck in it. "Superior Meats is closing. Now that she is the sole owner of the store, she doesn't want to manage the operation or live with the constant memories of her late husband."

"I wouldn't want to either," said one of the girls sarcastically.

"Who is she selling the business to?" asked Maria sharply.

"Ah, well, that is the problem. Mrs. Vieira is not selling the business, she is selling the building."

"What? She can't do that!" cried Maria jumping to her feet.

"I'm afraid she is," he responded. "She has also inherited the properties adjoining the meat market building, one on either side, and another one a few doors down. They are hers if she decides to sell." Mr. Tilson's voice was quavering and I wondered if he hadn't said too much.

In the hospital, Mrs. Vieira boasted she would be rich as a result of her husband's death. Being an addict to searching online real-estate properties, I knew that land in the downtown sector sold at a premium. The Superior Meats building alone spanned two property widths and the depth of the lots were about three. Together with the connecting properties, the square footage of the land would be substantial and could be sold as a parcel to developers for millions; a quicker and more lucrative means of return, by far, than from her husband's retail meat supply business.

Right across the board, the sales from red meat were diminishing. With the growing concern of growth hormones and the massive slaughtering of animals, I was buying less meat not only for the restaurant, but for personal consumption, as well. Chicken and fish entrees have substituted the heavy meat specialties that once dominated most restaurant menus. Although, at Walker's we still serve a freakishly large number of steak and frites. Sometimes you have to treat yourselves to sodium-injected cholesterol, nothing else will suffice.

Maria was fuming. She pointed to the group around her. "What about his employees? They haven't been paid last week's wages and haven't been given any prior notice of this sale."

"Your outstanding paychecks will be mailed to you and Mrs. Vieira will compensate all the employees with severance pay. I'm afraid she is not willing to reopen the store under any circumstances." His voice cracked. "Although I'm not really the one who should be telling you all this, I have been advised by Mrs. Vieira to speak freely — closure of the store is immediate. Your services are no longer required and her lawyers are handling your cases now. You should be hearing from them soon." His voice was almost gone.

The room of people seemed too stunned to answer. Louise was the first to speak. "Listen, everyone; I am very sorry for the men and women who are losing their jobs. This is terrible news and I realize it's a great shock for you all. But we must welcome Mr. Tilson as our new representative at City Hall. We are here to support changes in the market and should try to get beyond this to matters that concern us all."

"If you think we are going to sit here quietly after we have just been told we lost our jobs, then you're insane, Louise," Maria announced. "I don't care if they bulldoze this whole place now. Come on, girls, let's get out of here and find a drink." She grabbed her coat from the back of the chair and tied a tight knot in the silk scarf around her neck. Pulling the strap of a large purse over her shoulder, she made for the door.

"Okay if we come, too?" asked one of the butchers. A defeated manner had replaced the nonchalant attitude he had initially arrived with. I was guessing he had a family at home to feed, but could use a drink before he delivered the news.

The former employees scrambled to their feet and ran after Maria, leaving two empty rows behind. Mrs. Wong stood up beside me and said she was leaving, too. She felt sorry for the girls, said she didn't feel right about discussing the beautification of the market now. Maybe tomorrow would be better. Several others left, as well. Now there were only a dozen members left in the room and me sticking out like a sore thumb in the back row surrounded by vacant seats.

I tried to blend into my chair by pulling my head down between my shoulders blades. The collar on my shirt rose up to my ears. I peered out from my lapels to find Louise watching me. She zeroed in on me with beady eyes and asked pointedly, "What are you doing here, Blondie? This is a members-only meeting."

"Oh. Hi, Louise. I came as Mrs. Wong's guest." I pulled myself up. "She had to leave early. I hope you don't mind if I stay?"

"I can't imagine why this meeting would interest you. I heard your restaurant is closed. Your chef has been arrested, hasn't he?" Before I could answer, she continued, "It's his fault we are in this mess. If Tony hadn't been killed, his wife wouldn't be selling the business and all those good people wouldn't be losing their jobs."

"Hey Louise, that's not fair. My chef did not kill Mr. Tony and he is not responsible for the sale of Superior Meats or those other buildings. Why don't you accuse Mrs. Vieira for selling out before her husband's body is even cold? I'm not making a dime while my place is closed. The market people aren't the only ones affected by the murders." Angry at first, I instantly regretted speaking with such insensitivity.

What was I doing spying on the market people? The police had the power to investigate, not me. I looked around at the remaining guests and felt embarrassed. I stood and left out the side door of the church's basement.

It was more than a light rain now and I longed for my umbrella. I was reminded of poor Mr. Tilson's soaking-wet entrance. As I climbed up the cement steps to the street, I did the buttons up on my new wool coat, which was getting drenched, and made a run for it. The car was parked around the block in front of the fruit market. I had to pass Superior Meats on the way. A piece of the police blackout paper had slipped down the inside of the window glass, revealing a hole to look through. I stopped and put my face against the window. Pitch black. Not a single light was on inside the store, not even a dim glow radiating from the refrigeration units. I jumped when the wind blew a page of newspaper against my leg.

I crossed the street to get a better view of the buildings attached on either side of the meat store that

would be sold, as well. What the heck, I was already
soaked, a few minutes wouldn't make any difference.
The Vietnamese toy store on one side of Mr. Tony's was
already boarded up with a SOLD sign glued to its front.
The store on the opposite side had been closed for some
weeks and I remembered guessing what might go in there
next, never dreaming it could be condos. The area didn't
seem quite right for a condo development. Smack in the
middle of the market, it would be out of place. This is
how neighbourhoods changed without anyone noticing
until it was too late. The market was vulnerable and the
realtors knew it.

Empty storefronts didn't help. Half the time the
dingy stores were let out to tenants hoping to make a
living on inventory they bought sight-unseen off the
cargo ships. Merchandise weighed out in pounds was
packed in crates and dropped off at the docks. Most
vendors took what they can afford. The assorted goods
were displayed randomly on sidewalk tables meant to
lure curious shoppers inside. I've been drawn in to the
murky interiors before. A faux-leather purse or silk scarf
would strike my fancy, and claiming my prize from the
table, would take it inside to pay. Wind-up mechanical
toys, sundry canned goods, men's wallets, or satin purses
share the long, half-empty shelves. A hopeful face always
asks me to look around, perhaps I need something else.
After one minute all I would need was to get out of there.

I wished I knew what other buildings Anthony
Vieira owned. Mr. Tilson hinted there was one more on
the block ready to be sold. Over the pattering rain, a
murmur of voices rushed past me, but the street was void
of signs of life. Resembling a black-and-white glossy film
clip, I expected to see Jack the Ripper standing under a
street lamp haloed with mist. The street was desolate.
Still no sign of the owners, the voices grew more distinct,
closer, suggesting it was time for me to move along.

I almost took a header out in front of a fish store, righting myself with a jerk of my back and a little hop. The pavement was slick with rain and newly fallen leaves. A few flakes of silvery fish scale stuck to the sidewalk, which was reflective in the store's security light. Suddenly the rain came pelting down. I hurried to where I had parked my car, around the corner near the vegetable store. Jumping puddles and stepping into concentric waves of water pouring out of the gutter pipes, I had one last stretch of block to go. I was thinking I better call Rick.

Three men stepped out of an alley, the alley behind Eddie's grandfather's store, the one across from the cheese shop, the one down the street from Mr. Tony's. The one in which I was going to die.

chapter eleven

I wasn't kidding about having martial arts training. Three years of kick-boxing had made these long legs of mine good for something else besides the forgotten mini-skirts in the back of my closet. I didn't think I stood a chance against three men, but I'd give it my best shot. Then, when a light went on in one of the above apartments, I got a better look at my assailants. These guys had to be high on crack. One of them so was emaciated and confused I doubted he was capable of swinging his arm. The other two might be trouble.

I took up the trained stance and they stepped back, surprised. I guess they didn't expect me to go on the offensive, or, more realistically, it was the arrival of Louis, Eddie's grandfather, holding a two-by-four in his hand. Ten feet behind him, Eddie stood quietly in the shadows. Louis was unwavering. Clearly this wasn't the first time he had held a weapon, possibly an army stint back home in Portugal before the family moved to Canada. I had a better chance of surviving now. Together we divided their camp.

The weaker one drifted back into the shadows of the alley, leaving his buddies to fulfill their mission. Shoulders jousting tentatively, they stood their ground, deciding their next move. They weren't pros at this stuff and not beginners, either, making them all the more unpredictable. Louis stood stock still, club at the ready.

My concentration on assessing my best defence was broken by the "whoop whoop" of a siren. The unmarked sedan came to a screeching stop beside us, causing the men to flee like frightened rabbits. I almost felt sorry for them. Maybe because they weren't much older than my son. Detective Winn jumped out of the car and plunged into the alley. A minute later he returned.

"They're gone. Did they hurt you?" he panted.

"No. I'm okay, thanks to Louis here." I smiled and pointed behind me. "And Eddie, of course. Louis's grandson." Eddie flashed a wave and bolted back inside a doorway.

I introduced Louis and Winn to each other. Louis denied being able to provide a proper description of the men, and left hurriedly. I figured I owed him. Louis had come to my defence, maybe even saved my life, and if he didn't want to get involved it was okay with me; he's lived in the market for over sixty years, I'm sure he's used to minding his own business. Winn was acting mighty protective, though, and insisted on driving me home.

"I'm fine, honest," I pleaded. "My car is just up ahead."

He held on to my arm. "Listen. Just get in my car, okay? I think you could use a drink. You look awful."

Why were men always telling me how awful I looked? Okay, admittedly my wool coat smelled like an old goat, my shoes were caked with mud, and my hair was matted and hanging in strands down my face. Didn't I possess enough inner beauty to make up for a being a sloppy mess most of the time? Winn would surely see the real me shining through.

I insisted we walk, saying the night air would do me good and that I didn't feel like driving home alone just yet. My nerves were raw. Although the sky promised a deluge to come, the rain had paused briefly. As we crossed the Spadina Avenue corridor, the wind driving north from the lake cut through me like a knife. Winn grabbed my arm again, double-timing me along Dundas Street into a rain-soaked, bustling Chinatown.

Better dressed for the weather than me, Winn wore a police regulation-style raincoat with grey rubber material on the outside and cotton-insulated lining on the inside. I was so cold my teeth were chattering. He slipped one hand over mine and plunged them both into his dry pocket. I pulled my other hand up into my coat sleeve and wobbled close behind. He led me down a few steps to a tiny hole-in-the-wall Korean deli filled with other wet customers buying hot cups of green tea and steamed buns. I ordered two deep-fried spring rolls with a side of fried rice noodles and coffee. Winn ordered the hot, spicy soup for himself and a pot of green tea.

I guess he thought he was funny, criticizing my taste in foods. I knew the heart-clogging effects of deep-fried foods, but as I explained, it was comfort food and I needed all I could get.

"But listen," I said, "if you ever want to go head-to-toe in a food challenge, I'm ready. As most of my chefs have found out the hard way, I can determine the secret ingredient in any creation and am capable of selecting the appropriate spices and herbs to add or eliminate in order to perfect it. I can tell you the merits of every vegetable and fruit known to mankind. And not to sound too pedantic, if spinach is not slightly steamed, it prohibits the absorption of iron, rendering the widely held belief that raw spinach salads are good for you. Completely unjustified. I defy anyone to beat me at recognizing the refrigerator smell first and I know at a glance which cream is going to curdle."

"Okay, okay, I'm sorry. You don't tell me how to do my job and I won't tell you how to do yours. Oh, wait, you are trying to tell me how to do my job."

"I haven't said a word."

"What about your interference back at Daniel's house and the trip out east to his sister's? Not to mention getting yourself hurt at the C.N.E. and now running around the market looking for clues. I'm starting to worry about you. I don't have time for that."

I felt it was only polite to ignore that comment, considering he had just helped me out of a tight spot.

"May I remind you that it was your idea I get involved in the first place? You suggested I talk to Maria, and that's precisely what I was trying to do. By the way, what were you doing in the market? Are you following me?"

I studied him while he cautiously sipped his tea, wondering what he really thought about me. His wide, handsome face didn't give anything away. When he looked up and caught me staring at him, he smiled. I fought the urge to fall deeply in love.

"I don't have to follow you. You're everywhere I go, constantly underfoot, and I want you out of the picture. I'm sorry I ever asked for your help. It's dangerous, Liz, go home and relax."

"Detective …"

"David."

"Detective," I repeated, not willing to give in so easily. "You don't know a thing about me. How on earth can I relax when I'm in danger of losing my livelihood? Hopefully the health board will allow us to open soon, but my chef's name still hasn't been cleared and until it is, my restaurant is sitting under a cloud of suspicion. I need to clear our reputation. I need to get some answers."

He didn't respond.

"Please, David. I'm drowning here."

He swallowed a spoonful of soup and looked me in the eyes. "Legally I can't share information, but if you tell me what you were doing in the market, I'll tell you why I was there."

It was a start. I told him about the community meeting, giving him details of Mrs. Vieira's plan to close the store and sell out. I described Maria's immediate reaction of outrage toward the wife and the employees' stunned expressions of disbelief. I said that Louise wanted to bypass the emotional tension concerning the closure altogether and get on with the meeting. Then Maria's take-charge attitude over the group led to their unified departure.

"After Louise squared off at me, I left the meeting. I found myself standing in the pouring rain, wondering if Tony Vieira ever considered divorcing his wife for her infidelity and that's when I realized I wasn't alone. I have to tell you the market is scary at night. Why don't you have more police in the area?"

"We're working on it. We're trying to get the families to work with us, but it was tough going. Old school mantra, you know: 'Don't trust the cops.'"

I believed Winn had a difficult job. I saw Louis's reaction to his questions. "Did they trace the source of the rat poison back to the meat found in Daniel's car?" I asked finally.

"I wish," said Winn. "Then I'd focus on proving that Daniel was in league with Anthony Vieira all along. So far I still believe Daniel's innocent, incredibly stupid, but innocent. The only fatal poison we've been able to find was in Albright's stomach contents. None was found anywhere else, including Cecilia's stomach."

"How could that be? I saw her at the hospital today."

"What were you doing at the hospital?"

"I was visiting a patient. He was at St. Mike's, too."

He squinted at me for a second, thinking of a response and must have thought better of it.

I thought I better explain. "While I was at the hospital, I bumped into Maria, and, believing her father was in one of the rooms, met Mrs. Vieira. Small world, isn't it?"

"For you it seems to be," he said.

"Cecilia Vieira strikes me as a very robust young woman."

"That's one way of putting it. She scares the shit out of me."

"Yes, she has that way about her. She sure didn't look very sick," I said.

"Admitting her was a precautionary step. She didn't eat enough steak off Albright's plate to cause fatal poisoning. The hospital examined her thoroughly, but couldn't say anything definitive. Her vomit, expelled at the table, may have contained trace elements, but it was cleaned up by the staff before we could do an analysis. And why were you at the hospital again?"

"I was visiting Mr. Randolph. You know the customer who supposedly got food poisoning at the restaurant. Remember?"

"I see, just a coincidence, after all." He relaxed and explained about the poison. Mrs. Vieira might have consumed enough to make her ill, but not enough register.

"So the councillor was the intended victim and the wife's poisoning was accidental. Good thing she only took a bite of his steak," I said. "She's lucky — it could have been worse."

"Yes funny that, lucky indeed since we've already established she didn't eat red meat it's highly unlikely she was the real target."

"Daniel was the first person to tell me that. She sure likes chocolate though, when I saw her this afternoon she was stuffing her face full of it."

Winn nodded knowingly.

"Tell me why you were driving through the market tonight." I asked. It was his turn to provide me with information.

"I got a tip from Nathan," Winn replied, "the homeless guy who used to sleep in the meat market's doorway. The night Mr. Tony was killed, he heard screaming coming from inside the store and saw Maria lying on the floor covered in blood. He was responsible for flagging the patrol car down."

"Do you think he saw the murderer and is too afraid to admit it?"

"I doubt he saw much. He would tell me if he had. Not an easy life living on the streets, but it is his turf and he watches. Since the murder, he's been roughing it in an old garage in the alley behind the store. Seems he can't get the image of Tony's dismembered head out of his mind."

"Would you?"

"I've seen worse."

I could tell David wasn't grandstanding. I could only imagine the misery he waded through every day. I felt for him.

He sipped his tea before continuing. "Nathan became frightened when he heard the familiar voices of some particularly nasty thugs arguing outside the garage tonight. If they discovered his whereabouts they would steal his can of change from panhandling. It's not much money, but enough to buy him a pack of cigarettes. After they moved off, he crept out to the street to make sure they were gone. The alleys and backyards are a maze of shortcuts. He couldn't see the druggies anymore, but he knew they were around and desperate!

"He spotted you at the end of the street standing all alone outside Superior Meats. He recognized you as the restaurant lady and called me from a pay phone, warning me that you might be in for some trouble. He must really like you. A quarter is gold to him."

"That's sweet, but how would he know who I was? Somehow I doubt he's a regular at the restaurant."

Winn's eyes narrowed.

"Oh, I'm sorry, that sounded callous. I didn't mean it, I'm grateful really I am," I stammered, hanging my head. Winn touched my cheek gently with his hand.

"You've had quite a shock, Liz, it's all right."

I was startled by his touch and he withdrew his hand quickly.

"But like I said, Nathan watches. I did ask him how he knew it was you and he told me that he remembered everyone who's ever given him a handout. He's not a junkie, you know. He's just struggling with some mental-health problems."

"Yes, I remember. I gave him a couple of bucks last week for helping me carry a few bags to the car. I didn't need his help, but you know how it is. Anyway, so Nathan tells you things. Do you pay him for information?"

"Sometimes. Sometimes I get the boys to pick him up and loan him the 'hospitality suite' down at the station."

"Hospitality suite," I repeated.

"Sometimes he wants a bath and a good meal at our expense."

I didn't think Winn was going to offer a better explanation, but I had one more question I wanted to ask. Then I really had to phone Rick. "Could you find out for me who owns the real estate on Mr. Tony's block?"

"I can find that out, but so can you. Those records are open to the public."

"Well you'll be faster and I would appreciate it."

An idea that had been simmering for some time in my brain was ready to boil over. Maria had reacted vehemently to the announcement that Tony's wife was selling out and when I saw her earlier at the hospital she she had been crying. I know she needed money, but she could get a job anywhere, I was sure of it. She was young and pretty and

I think fairly intelligent. I would've hired her, for that matter. She could help in the kitchen or wait on tables; she'd certainly give Marlene a run for her money. What if Maria had more than just her job at stake? When I mentioned to her that I had been talking to Cecilia Vieira, she was truly frightened. I saw it her eyes. I had a startling revelation. At the same time, Winn's cellphone rang. He fished it out of his raincoat and answered, "Winn here, what is it?" He listened intently to the voice on the other end and said, "I'm at 1700 Dundas Street, south side." He flipped the phone shut with a snap of his hand. "I have to go," he stated, and stood up.

"What's wrong?"

"Police business, I have to get my car. I'll get a cruiser to drop you off at yours."

"I can find my way back by myself."

He leaned into my face and whispered. "Try not to deliberately piss me off, okay?"

chapter twelve

The road was glistening wet with halos of light dancing off the oncoming cars. Rain was coming down in thick sheets across my windshield and the wipers, turned to warp speed, were about to launch into hyperspace. I could see the rubber slipping off one of the blades, causing the metal arm to squeal every time it scraped across the glass and prayed anyone foolish enough to be out in this weather wouldn't be speared by one. Confident that the rain would keep the parking police busy counting tickets for their quotas back at the depot, I parked boldly on the street beside the restaurant. Kitty was caught briefly in my headlights before she scooted down the entrance to the alley. She was on a mission. So was I.

With my wool coat over my head, I ducked from the car to the front door, grabbed the door handle, and yanked hard. The handle almost came off in my hand, but the door didn't budge. I was getting tired of this. Ten years, seven days a week, from nine in the morning to twelve midnight, 364 days of the year, I've only ever closed for Christmas and now it seemed like I was always closed.

My keys were somewhere at the bottom of my purse and I started digging around for them, peering through the front window, hoping to see Rick — he's been known to sit in the dark. An older, sophisticated-looking couple strolled past. Noting my anguish, they commented that it was a shame such a nice place had gone out of business. And although I didn't say a word, they eagerly suggested a great new restaurant that had just opened around the corner. I thanked them and pretended to leave; better than killing them, I supposed.

When the coast was clear, I opened the door and locked it behind me. No point adding insult to injury by having people come in to use the washroom. I lit a candle in a wrought-iron holder instead of turning on the house lights and poured myself a glass of merlot from a resealed bar-back bottle. I looked around glumly and started to take it out on the restaurant. "This is your fault," I said out loud. "If I had a normal career, I wouldn't be in this mess."

When my eyes adjusted to the dim light, I saw a piece of paper pinned to the kitchen door. It was a note from Rick. I had just missed him. He had waited around for the inspector to arrive before the dinner hour, but to no avail. The inspector was unable to process the necessary paperwork until tomorrow morning. He was assured we could open the next day. The staff had been summoned for an 8:00 a.m. meeting and Daniel was coming back to work. Finally, a light at the end the tunnel.

I left my half-finished drink on the bar, blew out the candle, apologized to the restaurant for my harsh words, patted the bar affectionately, and jumped back in my car. I was going to Toscano's dance hall. If Maria was still rehearsing, and I bet she was, I had something I wanted to ask her.

I jockeyed round Toscano's parking lot, tucked behind the building, and found a space along the outer perimeter, near the rear property fence. A row of narrow backyards with covered barbeques and empty garden pots butted against it on the other side. The club was busy with dancers bustling in and out of the lot. I followed in the wake of a young couple dressed in matching sequined outfits moving rapidly along the sidewalk toward the front door. Before climbing the stairs to the tufted, padded-leather doors above, I stopped to admire the building's new cool slate-grey exterior with stainless-steel trimmings. Gone was the outdated purple stucco facade I remembered from long ago. Tonight Toscano's looked fancier than the nightclubs on Richmond Street.

A well-known landmark in the city, this popular nightclub was loved by young and old alike. Having survived fifty years in the central west end of Toronto, the neighbourhood club had recently undergone a massive renovation. I had heard a rumour circulating that not everyone approved of the new exterior — you can't please everyone all of the time — but the refurbished ballroom had maintained the same classic proportions inside, with brighter lights than ever before and a new barroom twice the size of the old one.

As part of the reopening ceremony, an international dance competition would draw a huge crowd. Offering a five-thousand-dollar cash prize for the best performance was destined to be a hit with the locals.

I assumed the rehearsal times were over by now since there was a small cover charge. I got my hand stamped by a woman who looked more like a gypsy fortune teller than an employee and walked into a central lobby, which was bustling with activity. The rain outside had left the streets empty and forlorn, but inside it was like Mardi Gras. I didn't feel conspicuous without a date. Tonight's ambience lent itself more to business than pleasure.

I wandered through another set of double doors that led into a narrow, glass rotunda. A circular waist-high wall, topped with spindle-shaped posts, overlooked a very crowded dance floor. This was the main ballroom. Some patrons stood behind the wall, observing and chatting about the dancers on the floor. I purchased a small tumbler of cold white wine and found a spot alongside a railing that was wide enough on which to rest my drink.

The perfect vantage point to watch the dancers, it didn't take me long to spot Maria. She was standing by herself in the middle of the floor. Other couples twirled and dipped around her. I thought she was alone until I noticed another dancer slinking in her direction. He stopped three feet away, swaying back and forth to the music with his hands flattened on his hips. At first Maria seemed to be oblivious to his presence. Then she stamped her foot and turned her back on him. Lunging at her with a high-kick step, he grabbed her long black hair in his fist. She spun around and lifted her hand to strike his face, but he caught her hand mid-air and pulled her whip tight to his chest. Bending her over backwards, he set her hair free, letting it sweep the floor until he lifted her straight up and into the air with one hand. My breath caught. The other couples made room as the two executed spins and thrusts around the room with electrifying precision and speed. They came to a show-stopping lift with Maria balanced high in the air, back arched, and her hips held tightly in the man's strong hands. I cried out, "Bravo, Bravo!"

I assumed the young man was Nicky, the dance partner Maria had mentioned at the hospital. He was pure heat and sizzling energy. His painted-on black nylon shirt and flared pants revealed a seductively lithe body that made me squirm in my shoes. From the looks on some of the other women watching from the sidelines it did to them, too.

Maria looked sensational. She was wearing the costume I had discovered tucked inside the gold bag along with the flyers back at the hospital cafeteria. When I had briefly handled the cloth, I felt a finely meshed nylon material. I didn't remember the glowing emerald fabric. The teensy outfit was stretched tightly across her small breasts and narrow hips. Feathers trimmed the hem and glass beads, surrounding the neckline, sparkled under the chandelier lights. It was a miracle of modern science that the skimpy dress, completely backless, didn't fall off when Nicky flung her across the dance floor.

As far as I was concerned, no one held a candle to Maria and Nicky. Every step, every movement, appeared effortlessly as one. There was only one other couple who stood out from the rest and like Maria, the girl in that duo was muscular and shapely, with noticeably pronounced tendons in her legs. Her hair was short and black, a pixie-cut. It was cute and it suited her, but was oddly different from the other women on the floor. Most of them either had long hair pulled into tight ponytails or swept up into grand architectural contrivances. Maria's was long and chestnut brown, but she wore it loose, with ribbons threaded through the heavy curls. Both girls' costumes were similar in brevity and style and the shoes had similarly thick, sturdy-looking high heels.

The other partner was shorter than Nicky and stockier. He moved like a tornado, kicking and hopping, spinning his partner endlessly. He was energetic and athletic, but hardly graceful or seductive. The two couples were obviously friendly and faked tripping each other as a harmless game. They were laughing and the usually aloof Maria was having fun. Good for her.

I looked at my empty glass and, still thirsty, went to

the bar. The ballroom floor had been replaced with new gleaming hardwood and the surrounding walls given a warm lustre of golden paint. The overhead chandeliers dazzled the eyes. A thousand teardrops of glass crystal had been refurbished or possibly just cleaned and I thought someday I'll try cleaning the office windows, when a fond saying of my mother's popped into my head, "Someday you'll be dead, too." The magnificent lights rose and fell slowly between songs.

The bar was absolutely gorgeous. I wished with aching heart I owned a bar like that. It was made out of oiled mahogany, with a glassy top and shaped like a key. Rows of liquor bottles were stacked at the far end in front of two massive, ornately carved mirrors suspended from the ceiling. There was an undulating surge of customers moving forward trying to get served. On the floor in front of the bar, five round tables had been pulled together by a group of young girls and boys chatting excitedly about tomorrow's contest. Separate tables scattered around the bar were full and the bar itself was packed shoulder to shoulder.

With this large a crowd, the bar was understaffed, causing the bartenders to fly up and down the key. Edging myself into a slot between two couples, I leaned against the bar, waited for a bartender to see me, and held my glass up, mouthing the word *water*. He nodded, not nearly as annoyed as I anticipated. Maybe the break from shaking one more pina colada or making change for another twenty to pay for a three-dollar soft drink was considered a welcome task. I gave him a buck, anyway.

The mirrors were tremendous in size. I could see all around the room and into the dance area. I could even see Maria and her friends leaving the dance floor and making their way toward the bar. Quickly, I ducked behind the woman with the big head standing next to me at the bar. She turned her back to talk to her husband and I found myself staring directly into a nest of teased hair trapped in a silver net with a velvet bow holding it in place. When the lady moved her head, I moved mine in unison.

Maria was going to get the idea I was stalking her if she saw me here tonight. I didn't want to have to explain myself to her and her friends. I thought if I could talk to her alone I could ask her what favours she did for her deceased employer. I got the impression his wife knew what they were and frankly I didn't think they were sexual.

I was looking for another way out and saw a fire exit sign posted at the top of a flight of stairs with an arrow pointing down. Below it was another sign indicating that the ladies' washrooms were also downstairs. Perfect, two birds with one stone.

Stepping down the rickety stairs, the basement seemed dilapidated compared to the rest of the newly polished club. The renovation appeared to have stopped with the completion of the front facade and main floor. It was postwar era down there. Overhead exposed pipes, connected to steaming radiators lining the hallway, disappeared through the wall and beyond to unknown mechanical rooms and storage spaces.

A freshly painted but severely scarred wooden door read LADIES ROOM, a twin door, on the opposite side, read CHANGE ROOM.

Naturally, when I peeked inside the ladies' washroom there was a lineup. I wondered if the dancers' changeroom had facilities and I pushed the door open like I meant it. One has to act like one owns the place for this tactic to work. I was in luck, nobody was in there. I went into a stall and closed the door. Just in the nick of time. Two women walked in the room right on my heels.

I recognized Maria's voice. I silently slid the bolt across on the stall door, opening it a crack to peek out, but a row of lockers that acted as a barrier between the toilets and the rest of the dressing room spoiled my view. I was about to close the door when the other girl approached a wash basin opposite me and splashed her face with water. It was the dancer she and Nicky had been clowning around with earlier. I heard Maria call her urgently, "Hurry up, Inez. Do that later. We need to make the exchange now."

"Exchange?" I whispered in surprise.

The girl called Inez turned around suddenly and looked my way. I gently closed the toilet door all the way and held my breath. I was sure she had seen me watching her. I could hear her move close to the door, waiting for me to come out.

"Hurry up, Inez. I hear someone coming down the stairs."

Inez went back to Maria and mumbled something inaudible. Pressing against the stall door I managed to overhear one word: "tomorrow." A locker door slammed, more whispering, and they left.

Two other girls came into the room. I flushed the toilet and stood in front of the sink, pretending to fix my hair in the mirror. Out of the corner of my eye, I caught something lying on the floor beside one of the lockers. I walked over and looked down. Remembering the deck of cards Maria had dropped at the hospital, I picked up the card and put it in my pocket.

I walked back into the hall and left through the rear exit door. The land was higher here on this side of the building and I stepped directly out from the basement level onto the paved parking lot. It was raining lightly. The lot wasn't as busy as it had been an hour ago. Some of the younger dancers had probably attended school that day, and, tired from a night of rehearsal and the excitement of the big contest tomorrow, they would want to get home to bed. Speaking of which, I was tired, too.

I had covered a lot of territory since this morning. I visited Mr. Randolph at the hospital where I met Mrs. Cecilia Vieira for the first time and talked to Maria in the cafeteria. Then I ate perogies at St. Lawrence market, met Mrs. Wong for the community meeting, almost got mugged in Kensington, and ate Korean in Chinatown with Detective David Winn, my hero. I visited my failing enterprise, complained bitterly about it (which I fully regret), and drove in the pouring rain to Toscano's to speak to Maria, which I was unable to do. Did I say I was tired? More like comatose.

To make matters worse, I had to be at the restaurant at 8:00 a.m. sharp for the staff meeting the next morning. I moved down an aisle toward my car. That's when I saw Maria's dancer friend, Inez, up ahead. She jumped into the passenger seat of an idling car. The car slowly backed up. Rather than passing behind it, I waited courteously for the owner to reverse out of the narrow space. It was a big car. The driver turned to gauge his room and as he neared I saw him. It was Detective David Winn.

He saw me, too. He stepped on his brake and I ran for my car. I jumped in and took off out of the driveway, bouncing off the curb with a slam dunk. After a few blocks I slowed down. Checking my rearview mirror, I realized he wasn't following me. Fine with me, I didn't want to talk to him, anyway. That's not true. I wanted to tell him the girl he was squiring around was in league with Maria. Some kind of an exchange could mean drugs. I shook my head. My mind was imploding and all I wanted to do was go home to bed.

Typically, I couldn't find a parking space at that time of night. So I left the car partially up on the curb in front of my house, a move guaranteeing I'd find a ticket stuck under the wiper in the morning. I had a room full of tickets. One more wasn't going to make a difference. I walked up the front path, noting that the house next door was pitch-black inside. My new neighbours moved in a month ago and the only glimpse I've had of them so far was when I got up one morning before dawn to pee. I heard a car coming to life out front and watched from my window, hidden behind the bedroom curtains, as four clean-cut men dressed like missionaries were boarding a black minivan with tinted windows. It was always so unnaturally dark in their house, I wasn't even sure they had their hydro hooked up yet. In contrast, my house always had a light on it somewhere. I've been known to wander at night, I hate knocking into things.

The neighbours on the other side of my house were ex-pat Lithuanian professors who dined every night at a filigreed cast-iron table covered with a white linen tablecloth. They drank frozen vodka from crystal glasses, talking more loudly of war as the evening wore on. I've been invited over many times and been fed Belgian chocolates while getting drunk on Kir. Good, bad whatever, Toronto is unquestionably a melting pot of diversity.

I walked in the front door of my house. Simultaneously, Jon called out to me from the kitchen.

"Hey, Mom, where have you been? I've been trying to get you on your cellphone for hours."

"Sorry, Jon, I turned it off." I sighed. He ambled into the hallway and leaned against the door.

"Boy, you look beat. Come into the kitchen, I have a surprise for you."

"Not now, honey, I'm exhausted and before I go to bed, I was wondering if I could use your computer."

"Can't right now, I'm defragging the hard drive and it will take a couple of hours. Leave a note for me and I'll do it tomorrow. Now come on into the kitchen, I have a surprise."

Too tired to argue, I hung my coat up on a peg to dry and wandered wearily into the kitchen. I thought my heart would stop. Sitting in the same chair where Winn had sat two days ago was Maritime Andy, drinking a beer, and looking very pleased to see me.

I can't say the feeling was entirely mutual. After our heated east coast encounter, I had invited Andy to visit me in Toronto whenever he liked. I never dreamed I'd see him a few days later in my kitchen.

Andy's pompadour hairdo and sideburns had been replaced with a stylish close-cropped haircut. He was wearing a simple black crew-neck sweater that exposed the collar of a crisp, white shirt beneath. Black khakis and tan walking boots finished the look. He looked good and I told him so. After the initial shock of finding him in my kitchen, I succumbed to his easy charm and decided I was happy to see him again. I also told him he could stay as long as he liked, meaning not more than a week, and made up the spare bedroom for him.

Andy brought me up to date on events back at the schoolhouse hotel. The big news was that Evelyn had successfully smooth-talked the painter into coming back to finish the job at the hotel and now they were dating.

He explained that, after hearing me prowling around on the fire stairs earlier and thinking the rest of the hotel was deserted, the painter decided to investigate on behalf of Evelyn, who was visiting her mother. He got considerably more trouble than he bargained for and Andy felt bad for tackling him.

"So it was him feeling his way along the walls." I said. I was relieved no one was trying to kill me, but was angered by the unnecessary scare. "Maybe you should have told him a late-night guest had checked in."

"I know, I'm sorry, but I knew he went to bed early so he could up at dawn to paint and I figured he'd be fast asleep. I didn't want to disturb him."

"Hello," I said, "not everyone falls asleep as easily as you think. Take me, for example. At least he was brave enough to check it out."

"That's what Evelyn thought, too. She's been fawning over him ever since."

"It's difficult imagining her fawning over anything. She looks as hard as nails."

"She's not hard and she didn't have to let you stay the night in the hotel, either." Andy was clearly offended. "The hotel was closed for renovation, but she was worried about you driving at night in the fog."

"Oh, Andy, forgive me, I've had a bad day. This revelation comes as quite a surprise and I should have thanked her. We'll talk in the morning."

Upstairs, in my bedroom, I thought about seeing David Winn earlier in Toscano's parking lot. Nice excuse, him telling me it was police business before bolting from the deli in Chinatown. After fuming for a while, I decided it wasn't his fault he was more interested in the attractive young dancer than me. Why not? From the looks of her, she probably didn't have food stains on every item of clothing she owned.

I hadn't fallen asleep fantasizing about anyone for a long time and figured there wasn't much point in me doing it tonight, either. Don't get me wrong, I was attracted to Andy, but he was seven years younger than me. Not enough to be criminal, but just enough to make that night at his house a one-time only kind of deal. I wasn't sure how he felt about me, either. I wasn't getting any obvious romantic signals from him. Maybe he was shy in front of Jon. I just didn't know.

Using the remote control, I turned on the television set, perched on an old parsons table, positioned at the foot of my bed. The last remaining piece of furniture I bought for my first apartment so many lifetimes ago, the well-designed table was still good as new.

Undressing, I took off my grey slacks, creased them with my fingers, and folded them over a hanger. The card, found in Toscano's dressing room, flipped out of the pocket and smacked the floor. Holding it up, I inspected it curiously. It looked as if it belonged to the same deck Maria had dropped and scrambled after in the hospital cafeteria. The jack of spades appeared on one side, soccer superstar Pelé's handsome face on the other. It felt heavy and thick, as if two cards were stuck together.

I picked at the top of the card where a slight gap showed, but I couldn't wedge my baby finger inside. I tried the nail scissors from the bathroom. It gave and split down the middle, revealing a small, hard piece of white plastic inside. It appeared to be a social security card. Red raised printing on the numbers and a blank where the name should have been. I wondered about the rest of the cards in Maria's deck. Considering the ramifications this presented, I'd have to tell Winn. The fact that I never wanted to speak to him again was clearly beside the point.

I stifled a yawn that would scare a rhinoceros, let alone a houseguest. I was still overwrought from the day's events and thought that watching television for a few minutes might clear my mind. First, I surfed the forensic shows, seen them all. Then the house and home renovation channels, seen those, too. I clicked up one more channel and hit a food show. Half asleep now, I searched for the remote that had disappeared in between the covers, but hesitated before turning off the television. The show was familiar and that puzzled me. I hated food shows. Then I remembered Cecilia Vieira.

chapter thirteen

I was the first to arrive at Walker's Way. Well not exactly the first. Kitty was waiting for me. I unlocked the door and got a good leg-rubbing in the process. Aw, she missed me.

I have shared many a problem with Kitty and even asleep she appears to hang off my every word. No doubt about it, I had a soft spot for her. So did Rick. He always left enough food and water for her in the basement. Regardless, we knew she could take care of herself. We had yet to discover her secret passageway. She never got locked in or out of the building, just came and went however she wished.

In return, I gave her a good scratching behind her bent ear and immediately washed my hands in one of the kitchen sinks. I hated to think where she's been. Rick arrived a few minutes later.

"Have you seen her latest trophy?" he asked, swiftly stepping aside so she wouldn't leave hair on his black pant legs.

"No, I haven't been downstairs yet. What did she bring home this time?"

"It looks like a coyote tail," he replied.

"Where on earth would she find a coyote tail?"

"Probably on a coyote," he quipped.

"Very funny."

"No, I'm serious. I saw one about a month ago driving home along Lake Shore. It was late and no one was around. We connected."

"You're weird."

"You don't know the half of it."

I smiled because that was probably true. "Kitty's tough, but I can't imagine her bringing down a coyote."

"Go down to the basement and check out her box of tails. Tell me what you think it is."

"I will later," I remarked. "It's not actually on the top of to-do list."

Rick chuckled. He had a theory about Kitty. He believed she was over-compensating for her own lost tail. When we first took her in, she had an oozing, bloody torn ear, and most of her tail was missing. Over the last two years she has collected a box full of assorted tails, mostly rats and squirrels, one raccoon, and now a mystery tail. We hoped someday she might find one to replace her own. In the meantime, I had to concentrate on the kitchen staff, who would be arriving any minute.

"I called Daniel and Michael to come in around nine this morning. They'll be here soon."

"I am here," said Daniel sweeping through the kitchen door, "and I can't wait to get started. Being cooped up with my sister was intense. Thanks for giving me another chance. I'll make it up to you both. You should see the special I have planned for today."

Michael and the legendary Ceymore, whom I refused to let Rick fire for the soggy pasta episode, waltzed into the kitchen together followed by two of the prep boys, plus the dishwasher. Rick and I left them to it. The radio went on full blast as soon as we left the room, signifying that the men were eager to begin. A controlled frenzy of activity would rock the kitchen until every food station was prepped and ready for service. Now that was music to my ears.

Rick and I went upstairs, but even before we reached the end of the hall we both knew something was wrong. The office door was damaged. Two of the locks were smashed and hanging off to one side. Luckily, one of the locks still held. Inside, we did a quick look around just to be sure nothing was missing. Truthfully, there wasn't anything worth stealing; the computer was ancient and the office furniture was even older. Of course, the safe was up here, but it was empty. Any cash that was in there a few days ago had already been deposited into my wallet. A thief wouldn't know that, though.

If I were a thief, I'd steal the booze we don't lock up, and enjoy myself on the house. Assuming of course, I had the foresight to leave before dawn. The cleaners arrived early one morning to find a burglar passed out on the bar with a forty-ounce bottle of vodka still clutched in his hands. The stereo was on, and a half-eaten plate of smoked salmon rested on his belly. This was one man's solution to the high cost of dining out; a new slant on "dine and dash" without the "dash."

Rick took stock of the damage and said he would pop down to the local hardware store to get a couple of new locks. While he was gone, I prepared a short speech for the staff. An hour later, I ambled back into the restaurant, ready for work. It was almost ten in the morning. A few of the front staff had arrived, half asleep and holding giant containers of take-out coffee. Waiters are not morning people.

Soon everyone was seated. I gave a heart-warming talk about how happy I was to see them again and sorry for the disruption in their schedule and how I was grateful that they hadn't decided to leave us for a restaurant that didn't employ murderers. Daniel looked stricken. A few of the staff giggled politely to cover the awkward moment. Perhaps it was too soon to joke.

I moved on. I had to remind Marlene that ours was a family restaurant and therefore when dressing for work to look like a waiter and not a stripper. I reminded all the girls that there should be no exposure of their bare midriff, especially those with pierced belly buttons. Skirts should be long enough for them to bend over a table without forcing mothers to cover their twelve-year-old son's eyes and that tops should *not* be see-through. Fairly straightforward, one would think. Unfortunately with no uniform code such as black pants and white shirts, the need for such restriction was necessary. This was still Queen Street West and I encouraged individual dress style that kept Walker's Way funky, not sleazy.

Standard rules applied. No blue jeans, no running shoes, and definitely no shorts or sandals. The male waiters naturally had less of a choice for apparel. I preferred casual shirts or golf shirts, not T-shirts. I reminded the boys to make sure they ironed their shirt or at least take it off before they slept over night at their girlfriend's place. It was a sad state of affairs when they returned the next day, wrinkles and all, without exchanging it for a new one.

Other points were sanitary ones, like washing hands regularly, no smoking on the premises, and no leaving half-eaten food behind the counter that might attract vermin. I was on a roll. Afraid I would turn on them in any minute, the kitchen staff started fidgeting. I was about to launch into what a fabulous job they were doing and release them mercifully from the meeting when the front door opened. Two uniformed police walked in, followed by Detective Winn.

"I'm sorry to interrupt this meeting, Ms. Walker, but we are here on official police business." He turned his back to me. "Daniel Chapin, you are under the arrest for the murder of Anthony Vieira. You have the right …"

Winn read him his rights while one of the policemen handcuffed Daniel's hands behind his back. Daniel looked at me with pleading eyes. I was too stunned to say a word in his defence. All I could manage was, "Not now, Detective, we're going to open in a couple of hours! Please, we need Daniel."

The policeman cuffing Daniel looked over at his commander. "I would appreciate your co-operation, Ms. Walker. Please allow us to do our job." He nodded at the officer, intimating that the restraints should be applied.

I followed Daniel and the police out the front door. Rick hurriedly instructed the staff to begin setting up for lunch. The sous-chef Michael practically ran into the kitchen. Catching up with Winn at the curb, I tugged at his arm. He turned and whispered to me, "Liz, I know this is a bad time for you, but it can't be helped. We have new evidence that implicates both Daniel and his sister. How would it look if I didn't take him in? I'm still not sure that it was Daniel who murdered Tony, but I think it could have been Meriel. We found her prints on one the glass refrigeration units in the store. We had to eliminate a hundred prints until we identified hers."

"That's not possible; she was on the east coast when Andy called her."

"No she wasn't. That's what we thought, too. After the crime geeks identified the print, I checked the flight Daniel was on to see what time he left. A ticket was issued in the name of 'D. Chapin' and someone did fly out on the morning after Tony's murder, only it wasn't Daniel. The description we got from the airline check-in was of his sister. Meriel's middle name is Danielle and using the same initial as her brother threw us off. She was still in

Toronto when he called her and he swears she was at home. Daniel didn't fly out until later on that afternoon. It seems both of them are lying. We are holding Meriel at the police station, too. Sorry, it doesn't look good for either one of them."

I couldn't allow myself to think about the scene in the parking lot last night. I locked eyes with him and begged, "Can you tell me more?"

"I'll call you later. I promise."

So, all along Daniel had been holding something back. Meriel must be one hell of an actor because I still believed she knew nothing about the murder. At her house in Portsmith, she gave me the impression that he was genuinely sickened by the details of the crime.

I suddenly remembered my earlier fear that Cecilia was in serious danger. I had been too preoccupied with reopening the restaurant to mention it to Winn. One good thing, if Meriel killed Tony and she was in police custody, then Mrs. Vieira was safe.

The day was not starting out the way I had intended. My chef was gone again and the health inspector turned out to be a real stickler. He was not only late, but dilly-dallied with his inspection, sticking thermometers in everything from hamburger to humus and getting in the second cook's way. There was no apology for closing us down and he had a huge chip on his shoulder for the hospital's error; a tick in his flawless record of closures. When he saw the cat's food bowl in the basement, he brightened. He told me in no uncertain terms to get rid of the cat.

I said, "What cat?"

"You are not allowed to have pets on the premises, Ms. Walker. I could give you a citation and another red if you're not careful."

"Listen to me you miserable … hey!" Rick poked me hard in the back with the tip of his finger.

Between pressed lips of a forced smile he rasped in my ear, "Keep your eye on the prize, Liz!" He then stepped in front of me, blocking my line of sight. He began to dazzle the inspector with a heart-felt dissertation concerning the difficulties that an inspector's job entailed. I left him to it.

As for Kitty, it's not like we sprinkle catnip in the hamburger and let her run loose. Everything is put away at night and she's never around during the day. If she is, she's either fast asleep from a long night of tail-hunting or with me in the office pretending to listen as I drone on. She keeps the restaurant rodent-free without using tons of toxic poison. Mice and rats develop a stomach for poison eventually and what doesn't kill them makes them fat. When they do die in between the walls or under the floorboards, they stink for days, a smell reminiscent of stale popcorn or dirty socks, not very appetizing.

It wasn't easy but we opened for lunch without Daniel. Rick obtained the green pass and placed it in the window. The kitchen was fully prepped with enough salmon specials for fourteen covers and twenty pastas du jour. That would normally be enough to get through a regular lunch, but it turned out to be as busy as a Saturday on a teacher's convention weekend. Evidently the old adage is true: bad press is better than no press.

The kitchen was plating orders as fast as humanly possible. Michael was earning his stripes; Daniel had trained him well. Still, with one man short at the stoves, a lot of tables had to wait longer than was acceptable. At one point I had to jump in to save Marlene from a table of impatient office workers ready to walk out. I comped a few drinks and engaged them in witty banter to take the edge off their hunger. That's about the only time I play the owner card. Normally, I never let on. When unexpectedly confronted, I have been known to point to the person standing closest to me and claim they're the owner. The older employees, having been left in this awkward position one too many times, have learned to conveniently disappear, leaving the inexperienced behind to cope.

Imagine the cleaning lady's surprise when I introduced her to the agent from Niagara Estate Wines as the owner and then fled like the caped crusader out the back door. I saw her leave a few hours later, dragging a shopping bag full of free samples.

We got through lunch, but dinner was going to be a much larger problem without Daniel. He had planned on working a double. I called in an old debt from an ex-chef buddy of mine who had lectured with me at one of the graduating chef schools. Bless his heart, he promised to come in with his own team for a few hours since his restaurant was closed for a television special makeover. My team would be exhausted by then, only too grateful to step aside.

I felt like hosting and greeted the faithful lunch regulars and guests with gusto. There's nothing like working your tail off to mellow you out. I was having fun listening to Rick joke about my hosting technique, a fine balance of obsequious hand-wringing and feigned subservience. Relaxed in the back booth, I was enjoying a tumbler of Scotch.

Then Winn walked in.

He had deep fatigue lines around his mouth and his eyes were dull. He managed a smile for me, momentarily lifting the gloomy aura he had brought in with him.

"Bad day at the office?" I asked.

"I've had worse, but I can't remember when. How about your grand opening?" he asked sincerely.

"Busy," I told him.

"Well that's good. Looks like you're putting your feet up. Mind if I join you?"

"If I said yes, would it matter?" I was still hurt after seeing him drive off with the attractive young dancer from the club.

He slid into the booth's seat opposite me. "I want to explain about last night, but there are private police issues I'm not allowed to discuss with you."

I'm such a pushover, maybe it was only a police matter, after all. I wanted to believe him.

"Why don't you have a drink? I just finished one and I don't mind having another."

"You driving?" he asked.

"Take the badge off for a minute, Winn. I won't be going home for a while yet. I have to clear a few things off my desk. What will you have?"

"I'll have a Scotch straight."

I walked around the bartender, who busy was washing the old ice down the drain and wiping off the sticky house bottles in the rail, saying I would help myself. We didn't close between lunch and dinner as many restaurants in the area did, but each bartender left his section clean and stocked for the next shift. I poured a refill and two good fingers for the policeman. Winn took a cautious sip and then belted the drink down in one gulp.

"Thanks," he said, "I needed that."

"I'm glad you're here, Detective. First, when is my chef coming back? And second, I think Cecilia Vieira may be in danger."

He looked at me pointedly.

"I'm sorry. You must be getting pretty tired of me interfering by now."

"Not really, I'm getting used to it. And please, I think you should start calling me David."

"Deal, I don't know about you, David, but I'm hungry. The chef is making me something special. Why don't we share?"

Our meal, which would cost hundreds of dollars anywhere else, was tailored-made to meet the simple, but satisfying bistro fare Walker's was well-known for. Instead of foams, fusions, and dreaded frisée, we were served old-fashioned rack of lamb, perfectly pink, leaning against a mound of whipped garlic potatoes, drizzled with tarragon oil, and surrounded with a scoop of mint pea mash. Winn looked like he died and went to heaven.

Over coffee, we talked about Daniel and his sister. Winn didn't believe that Daniel had it in him to murder anyone, but he wasn't so sure about Meriel.

"She has admitted that she knew Tony previously. He was a junior salesman for a large outfit in Nova Scotia before he set up shop here. Their mother operated a diner on the coast and he tried to push discounted meat on her."

"The diner was called The Sea Biscuit," I informed him.

"That's nice," he said sarcastically.

I smiled. "You were saying."

"He sold her discounted meat, the kind that falls off the back of a truck, if you know what I mean? The company caught onto his scheming and attempted to charge him for stealing, but he was young and a circuit judge gave him a slap on the wrist instead. He's had a personal vendetta against the Chapin family ever since."

"Why blame them, why not the company who fired him?"

"Mrs. Chapin caught Tony cornering her daughter in the fridge locker. She was only sixteen at the time. The father had died the year before and Daniel was just a kid. Their mother was worried about Tony hanging around and complained to the company. This came at the same time they were questioning his integrity. He was fired and no one on the coast wanted to hire him after that. Gossip spreads fast out there, I take it."

"That's probably when he moved to Toronto," I said, "and yet I never got the feeling he was crooked. I dealt with him for years."

"Obviously he learned to be more discreet. He has four other stores spread across Ontario and I think he was planning on widening his operation, and then somehow he found out his new partner was sleeping with his wife and he went berserk."

"I know that's what Daniel thinks, but I have a feeling there's more to it. Tony might have been jealous, but his reaction to his wife's affair was over the top. I think money was involved and losing his wife was the straw that broke the camel's back."

"If you're talking about real estate, we are looking into the frequent land transfers that have been occurring in the area in the last year. No ties to Tony yet, but we're working on it."

"Meriel freaked when Daniel said he was involved in a business opportunity with Anthony Vieira. Daniel wouldn't have been aware of any previous history between them. He was too young. When Daniel started at Twister's, Tony must have recognized the family name. Along with the family resemblance, the two of them are strikingly similar."

"That's what she told us, too. She knew her brother was in over his head and admits coming to Toronto to confront Tony. She swore she would go to the police if he was involved in anything illegal. She really hated Vieira, but she says he was alive when she left him in the store that night."

I thought about that. "Meriel wasn't the only one who hated him. It seems he made a habit of hurting the women around him. Maria found him repulsive and it's no secret his wife is happy he's dead. And that reminds me, I think you should keep an eye on her. Cecilia Viera stands to inherit a fortune in property. Maybe someone might find it advantageous to kill her, too."

"We're keeping a watchful eye; I don't want you to bother her." I was about to protest, but Winn put the palm of his hand over my mouth. I gave it a big, wet lick. He instantly withdrew his hand and waved it in the air. "Yuck, where'd you learn to do that?"

"I raised a child, and it got your hand off, didn't it? Never do that again and stop telling me what I can and can't do. I asked you before about what properties she inherits. If you know, why don't you tell me?"

"Because you might jump to the wrong conclusion, I like to take things slowly. Now, as I was saying, Andy swears his sister wasn't in the meat store when he arrived that night and found Tony sliced and diced. He does confess he was at the cattle show the day you got struck unconscious. He left after he talked to Martin Wright and asked that he contact you. You know that part, of course. After Daniel loaded the meat and discovered the bloody packages inside, he went home, packed, and booked a flight out east. He didn't leave as quickly as he said he did, though. We know his flight wasn't until four o'clock in the afternoon the next day. This gave him enough time to drop by the convention centre, before you were attacked. He now admits going there to pick up his equipment. When your former employee, Martin Wright told him two guests were taken away to the hospital and the police were involved, he knew he didn't want to hang around."

"Daniel admitted to me he went back to get his knives. Chefs are very possessive about their tools. Just one of those hollow-edged blades can cost two or three hundred dollars." I knew in fact the blade was strong enough to cut through bone and muscle. "Do you think it was Daniel who called the cops to fish me out of the Dumpster?"

"No. He says he didn't even know you were hurt. He was gone by then."

"So who did call the cops?"

"I don't know. But whoever did; they saved your life."

"Don't remind me."

Winn asked if we could go to my office and talk privately. The staff was trying not to be nosy, but I felt their eyes on us, too. Following closely behind me up the stairs, he must have been looking at my ass because there wasn't much else to see. With another light blown out in the hall, it was even darker than usual. I fumbled with one of the new locks Rick had installed earlier after the break-in, inviting Winn to push against me, his breath warm on the back of my neck. I managed to open the door before my legs buckled under me. We weren't in the office a second when he pulled me to him. We crossed the floor in unison, me back stepping until my body was pressed against the fireplace. He pushed harder against me, burying his face against my neck, and began kissing my throat. He lifted my hair with one hand, brushing the back of his hand against something and stopped abruptly.

"Where did you get this?" he shouted into my ear. He grabbed Daniel's apron off the mantle.

"David, what's wrong?" I pleaded.

"Where did you get this?" he repeated.

"It's Daniel's. Rick found it in the kitchen and brought it up."

"We've been looking everywhere for an apron like this. Heavy fibres from a butcher's apron were found in one of Tony's severed hands. This one has been torn precisely as we suspected the missing one would be. We checked all the butcher's aprons for traces of blood and could only come up with animal blood. They were ruled out."

I saw the tear in the apron. I could see light-coloured threads exposed against the black surface. I was beginning to have doubts about Daniel myself.

"I have to take this to be tested right away. We had the knives in for analysis, but they were clean of human DNA. It looks like your chef might be guilty after all. I bet he's been looking for this, unless he gave it to you to hide."

"How dare you!" I snapped. "If, he gave me his apron to hide, I wouldn't leave it out here in the open. Rick was wearing it to clean up the kitchen after we were shut down and I was waiting for Daniel to come back to retrieve it. They're expensive to buy, you know."

Then I remembered the failed burglary attempt. I told Winn about it.

"You're telling me you had this all along?"

"I don't know what you mean by all along. I didn't know you were looking for it. I told you Rick found it downstairs. It doesn't prove Daniel killed anyone. There's no motive, Winn, you said it yourself."

"It doesn't prove he didn't, either. The connections between you and Daniel are growing. I've asked myself a million times why you would fly out to Halifax to talk to him before the police had a chance. Finding his torn apron up here was one more reason to suspect your involvement. Maybe you two have a history, after all. I told you before I'll charge you with obstruction if you get in my way."

I started to cry. Blubbering, with big wet tears rolling down my cheeks, I told him to get out.

"What are you crying for?"

"I don't know."

"Liz, I'm sorry, please calm down. I had no right to raise my voice." He walked around the desk and took my hand. "I'm tired and I'm this close to solving nothing. I don't know who killed Mr. Tony, I have no idea who poisoned Mr. Albright, and I thought the two persons I have under arrest were not guilty of anything except duplicity. I've got to take this apron in to the lab immediately. I'll call you later with the results."

chapter fourteen

I plopped down on my chair and pushed a pile of bills off to the side of the desk. Putting my head down on the fake wood grain, I replayed the scene before Winn discovered Daniel's apron. Blood was pounding in my ears. I opened my purse, searching for an aspirin, and noticed the white plastic card tucked in a pocket of the lining. Shit, shit, and double shit, I had forgotten all about it. Winn would kill me for not showing him this. The phone rang, and, thinking it was him, I practically jumped on it. Never disappointed to hear my son's voice, I'd still have felt a lot better if it had been Winn.

"Mom, I got that information you asked me for last night."

"What information?"

"Remember, you came home and asked me to look it up on computer, but I was defragging the hard drive?"

I didn't respond.

"The property records for the City of Toronto. I got the ownership names."

I perked up. "Oh!"

"There are four properties listed under the ownership names of one Anthony and Cecilia Vieira. Three addresses in a row and one on the other side of the alley. The last address was originally owned by a Mr. Alex Kozinski. It was the first property to change hands. The others have been in the last year."

"That can't be right. Are you sure?"

"The record says it sold two years ago to the Vieiras. Who's this Kozinski guy?"

"That's Louise Kozinski's father. He started the cheese store over fifty years ago. I assumed she inherited it after her father died."

"What store are you talking about?"

"The Cheese Emporium, where I get the spicy vegetarian paté you like. Is there anything else?"

"It says it was sold publicly as an estate sale."

"Isn't an estate sale when the bank sells a property due to a mortgage foreclosure?" I asked rhetorically.

"As a last resort, I think it is. I mean a bank isn't in the real-estate business. If you default for too long in your payments and can't get an extended loan, the bank has no choice."

"Well, dear, I'm glad you're so sympathetic toward the bank. Wait until you get old and bitter like me."

"You're not old, Mom. A little bitter, perhaps," he joked.

"Who will you tease when I'm not around?"

"Are you leaving? Great, I'll have the place all to myself."

"Be careful what you wish for, sonny. Anyway, I'll be home soon. Tell Andy I'm on my way. And by the way, thanks for not asking."

"Not asking what?" He was toying with me.

"About Andy. I'm not sure how I feel about him staying at the house. Are you all right with it?"

"Mom, it's your house. And it's your life. You decide."

"I invited him to the dance contest before I left the house this morning. Are you and Susan interested in going? You might be able to buy tickets at the door?"

"I showed her the flyer. She said she'd rather watch it on the local news. I don't think she likes dancing and apparently it's going to be broadcast live. I think it's sold out, anyway. You're lucky you got tickets. "

I hung up, wondering how serious he was about the police rookie. Ironic that mother and son were both attracted to the fuzz. Ha, there's a word you don't use anymore, not unless your name is Shaft and you star in a 1970s cop show. I continued to stare at the phone as if it would ring again and tell me more. Ten minutes later I dialled Winn's number, but his voice mail was full. I would tell him about the card at the dance tonight. I figured he'd be there since he knew Inez. It's possible he was trying to get information on Maria by befriending her. He didn't think twice about asking me to help. I easily volunteered, maybe she did, too.

I forgot the Blue Jays were playing a home game. Access to the Gardiner, via the Rogers Centre, was jammed. Greyhound busses, parking queues, and ticket hawkers blocked the roads. I made a U-turn and drove home east, all the way along Queen Street. An unbearably slow drive made worse by traffic lights at every street corner and wayward pedestrians pretending to be pigeons. I got stuck behind a streetcar and wished I could hook my car to it. I didn't want to go to the dance tonight. I wasn't really interested in going anywhere except to sleep, but I didn't want to disappoint Andy, either. A Latin dance competition was sure to make his trip memorable and I felt I owed it to him.

Queen Street stretched east to west, much like

Lake Shore Boulevard, except it ran through the city in a straight line parallel to Lake Ontario. The street linked diverse, back-to-back communities, which one could distinctly describe as, rich, middle-class, up-and-coming, poor, and dog-eat-dog.

I made it home to my up-and-coming neighbourhood in good time. Compared to a weekday, the Saturday rush hour was shortened by half. By the time I reached home, I even managed to talk myself into wanting to see the dance and decided my detective pal should be made aware of my new concerns. I was getting all dreamy-eyed, remembering our romantic interlude before Winn discovered the apron. Hurrying through the front door, my head in the clouds, I made the mistake of not watching where I was going. I fell over a gigantic duffel bag. Words that could peel paint shot out of my mouth, and when I sat up, I found Jon and Andy staring down at me.

"Mom, are you okay?"

"Of course I'm okay. What's that stupid bag doing there?"

"Sorry, Liz, that's mine. I got an acting job in New York and I'm leaving on the red-eye express from the island tonight after the show." I reached out for Andy's hand and he pulled me to my feet.

"Well that explains Elvis's absence."

"What do you mean?"

"Nothing — are you sure you want to go to the show?"

"I wouldn't miss it for the world, but I do have to leave right after. I'm already dressed and it's getting late. You better change and we'll head downtown."

Woe is me and I just got home. In any case, Andy said he'd drive and although I don't trust many people behind the wheel, he had already proved his driving skills back on the east coast. In truth, I loved being a passenger. I got to look at all the pretty lights.

I changed into a black, lacy cocktail dress with a matching bolero jacket, shoved my feet into a pair of satin high heels, and brushed my teeth. Did a twirl in mirror. *Not bad*, I thought. I checked my watch. Now that I was dressed, I had time to call Louise Kozinski. The Cheese Emporium's phone number was filed under "caterers" in my suppliers' directory; Louise made cheese platters for every occasion. Her home number was jotted in pencil beneath.

Following in the wake of the streetcar, I considered the information Jon gave me about her store being sold in an estate sale. Losing the store her father owned and operated for over fifty years must have been unbearable. Louise had to have been nearly bankrupt to be unable to prevent the bank from selling her property. I know she lost her husband to cancer a few years ago and although the government paid for most of the treatment, there were still out-of-pocket expenses. She couldn't earn much in the cheese shop with business steadily declining over the years, thanks to villains like Albright and Tony.

Did she hate them enough to kill them both? I wondered how she felt about Cecilia Vieira now that the properties would be sold and torn down. Louise had probably spent her whole life in the market. I'd be beside myself if I were in her shoes. Although, I had to admit, she looked pretty cool at the meeting after she found out about the impending sale. Then I remembered what had been plaguing me for the last week.

A butcher's apron was hanging on a peg behind the heavy fridge door at the Cheese Emporium. I saw it in there when Louise lifted out the block of cheese for my order. That's why I noticed her maroon jersey dress the morning after Tony's body was discovered. Normally her street clothes would be covered by the protective apron. She only removed it before coming around the deli counter to tempt new customers with a free tidbit.

She didn't come around the counter to give me freebies anymore. I had eaten my quota of handouts, so it hadn't been removed it on my account.

The apron was a gift from her late father. She always hung it around her neck when slicing cold cuts or cheese, a valued lesson learned from her father when she was eight years old. Standing by his side, she waited for the paper-thin slices of proscuitto he carefully sliced for a school sandwich, when his cleaver slipped off the bone and punctured his stomach. The day she recounted this childhood memory to me, she gripped the rubber apron with both hands. It had been repaired, too.

I picked the phone up to call Winn at his office. It was no surprise that he didn't pick up. He was probably setting up a firing squad for Daniel and his sister outside in the precinct's parking lot.

I left a message on his answering machine, telling him of my new suspicions.

Louise had the motive, and she had the ability. She was strong, knew how to handle knives, and most importantly, had a butcher's apron just like Daniel's. If her apron was still hanging on the inside of the cooler, then it needed to be tested for blood before it disappeared.

Tony's widow had been released from the hospital and might also be in danger. Louise might have had knowledge that Tony was planning on selling the property she cherished, along with the others on the street. He would have destroyed the only life she had ever known, so she got rid of him only to find out his wife would do the same thing, too. Louise wouldn't have long to go before she was expelled, banished from her childhood home forever.

I was about to give up after six rings when she answered the telephone. She was out of breath. "Hello."

"Hi, Louise, this is Liz Walker from Walker's Way restaurant. How are you?"

"Considering the market is half dead with no business, not very good. I'm sorry for not being very nice to you at the meeting the other night, but I was upset."

"That's not why I'm calling, but thanks."

"I'm not open for business at the moment, either, so I can't fill any orders for you. Besides, I thought you were closed."

"Walker's is open again. I wanted to ask you something about your store."

"Like what?" Her voice hinted at annoyance and I knew she wasn't going to like my question, but I had to let her know I was on to her.

"I wondered where you would go when your building was torn down and the condos go in. Maybe Tony's death hasn't worked out for you, after all. Has his wife already given you notice. Is that why you're closed?"

"Who says my building will be torn down? Don't believe everything you hear. Actually, I'm closed because I have a few ..."

Before she could answer, I could hear chimes sounding in the background.

"Sorry, there's someone at the door, hang on a minute."

Louise's footsteps could be heard crossing the floor. I visited her apartment many years ago and was familiar with the layout. There was a living room at the front overlooking the street, two bedrooms in the back, and a kitchen and dining room in the middle. A joint hallway that connected the rooms and the stairs from below opened into the hall through a door that was kept closed to limit the drafts. I heard her open the door and call out, "Who's there?"

Her heavy footsteps sounded hollow as she climbed down the old, wooden stairs leading to the side door. I heard muffled voices and a minute later the voices drew clearer. Louise had company. She picked the phone up and said, "Sorry, Liz, I have to go. You'll

never guess who's dropped in. Cecilia Vieira is here."
And she hung up.

I talked Andy into driving over to Kensington before
we went to the dance. Although this would make us
late for the opening ceremonies, I wanted to make sure
Mrs. Vieira was safe. I didn't want any blood on my
hands. Winn's cellphone was turned off and he still
didn't answer at the station. I was thinking the guy
should own a restaurant; he was harder to get in touch
with than me.

It was just after eight o'clock and the market was
closed up tight. I could see lights shining in the upstairs
apartments over a few of the shops, but not Louise's. Her
front drapes were open, allowing me to see that the front
room inside was dark. When I asked Andy to wait in the
car, he said, "No way, not this time," and accompanied me
closely, very closely, down the narrow passage leading to
Louise's private side entrance. Three feet in, we couldn't
see a thing, making it necessary to feel our way along
the brick wall with our hands. My eyes adjusted and I
detected a faint glimmer outlining a door. Andy saw it,
too, and nudged me ahead. We had almost reached it
when a security spotlight was triggered, blinding us with
bright light. I yelped and jumped backward, banging into
Andy's chest. He laughed out loud, holding me tightly
around the waist.

"Shhh," I said, easing out of his grip.

"You're the one who screamed," he whispered back.

"Never mind, look at this." I pointed out that the
aluminum screen door was partly open and a half-torn
flyer was stuck in the frame.

"What is it?"

"It's a Toscano's flyer like the ones I saw Maria with
at the hospital."

Andy knocked on the inside door and it swung open easily. He stepped inside a small foyer at the bottom of the stairs and I could tell he was listening. He knocked harder.

"I don't hear anything. Should we go up?" he asked.

"I don't know. The door shouldn't be open like this. Let's check it out just in case."

Upstairs was quiet except for the ticking of an enormous grandfather clock that greeted us in the central hallway. I find ticking comparable to Chinese water torture. Beautiful craftsmanship or not, if the clock lived with me I'd have dismantled it by now.

The rooms at both ends of the hall were dark, but the kitchen light was on. I peeked in with Andy's head close to mine. Pieces of a broken teapot lay across a saturated tablecloth, a kitchen chair was on its side, and torn pieces of paper were strewn across the floor. Andy and I looked at each other and then he turned.

"Where are you going?" I whispered.

"I'll check the bedroom. You look in the living room."

Thankfully, no one was hiding in the front room ready to pounce. I returned to the kitchen and picked up one of the larger scraps of paper off the floor. It had clearly been torn from a legal document and if I wasn't mistaken it was Anthony Vieira's signature scrawled across the bottom. I've never seen his signature, but it was easy to read. Mine looks like a polygraph on acid. I knelt down on the floor and arranged the few pieces big enough to read but other than the words "Will and Testament" it didn't tell me anything.

"No bodies in the bedroom, but look what I found." Andy held out his hands, which contained tiny, white, cut pieces of plastic. I took a couple and tried fitting them together. Some of the pieces looked yellowed, and some had numbers and partial names.

"You're looking at these things like you just saw a ghost. What are they?"

I pulled out the card I had in my purse and showed it to Andy. The man wasn't stupid and he quickly dumped the rest of the pieces in his hands onto the kitchen table and began putting them together, literally and figuratively. There was about ten complete cards altogether, including the one I had, which made eleven.

"You want to tell me about this?"

"I'm not sure I can. I found a card like this between two playing cards on the floor in the change room at Toscano's dance club.

"When was this?"

"Last night. I wanted to talk to Maria at the club, or at least I thought I did, and then I changed my mind. I thought she'd think I was a nut job if she thought I was following her." I didn't want to tell him about my earlier arrangement with Detective Winn to watch her. "I saw Maria earlier at the hospital. She dropped a deck of playing cards and got very nervous about me touching them. I'm pretty sure the playing card I found this hidden in was from the same deck. I suspected there were more."

"And here they are," Andy said. "I can only think of one reason why anyone would have all these cards, although they're useless all cut up like this. Someone didn't want them in circulation." As I said the man wasn't stupid. "We better not touch anything else. Let's get out of here. You might want to get in touch with your police friend as soon as possible."

I agreed. I should have told Winn about my suspicions of Louise before this, but he was so excited about the apron yesterday that I didn't get a chance.

"I'll tell Detective Winn as soon as we get to the dance. If he's there," I added.

chapter fifteen

Dufferin Street was blocked by a police barricade and emergency vehicles crowded both sides of College Street. I experienced vertigo if I turned the bathroom light on and off too quickly and the red and yellow rotating flashing lights were giving me a headache. A policeman, who looked vaguely familiar, was dutifully directing a lava flow of cars into a state of side-street mayhem.

I rolled down my window to ask if a fire was causing the delay, but he pointed his finger and waved us on. I informed him that we were going to Toscano's and asked him where we could park. The policeman stopped directing the pedestrians for a moment and said testily, "I'm not a parking attendant, lady." But then he stared straight at me. "I remember you. I'm on traffic duty for a month because of you."

Recognition dawned. He was the sergeant on duty back at Daniel's garage. Winn had commanded him to escort me to his cruiser, but I had slipped out of his grip and ran back to find the trunk full of rotten meat. At the time, I was unfamiliar with the detective's methods, but it soon became clear he wouldn't tolerate carelessness from his men.

I turned to Andy. "Floor it."

I had to find another way to get inside Toscano's and find Winn. Andy let me out about a block away and agreed to find someplace to leave the car where it wouldn't be towed. Then he would catch up with me outside the club.

It was starting to rain again and getting cooler. I was in heels and wearing a cocktail dress, definitely not dressed warm enough to hoof it down the block to the club. Before Andy drove off, I grabbed an old trench coat from the back seat of the sedan and a pair of rubber boots. I also found my old camera sitting amongst a lost-and-found collection of paperbacks, umbrellas, and assorted pieces of odd clothing, not customers — but mine — piled in a heap.

The camera had been rolling around in the back seat of my car for months. I meant to take the film in to be processed, but there was still one picture left on the roll. I ripped off a long-lost glove stuck to the camera's Velcro strap, put it on, and strung the camera around my neck.

While another security cop concentrated on crowd control, I scooted around the caution tape. No one wants to be in a train wreck, but you can't help looking if there is one. Morbid curiosity seekers were keeping him busy.

I mingled in with the press, hoping my weighty camera would give me a professional look. State-of-the art digital photography was out of my league and I prayed no one would notice. The same traffic cop who recognized me had rotated duties and was now guarding a roped area. He spotted me and walked in my direction. I flashed a bulb in his face, blinding him long enough for me to blend further into an ever-increasing number of media hounds. The camera made a soft whir as it rewound.

The crowd let out a collective gasp. I poked my head through a gap of onlookers to see a stretcher being hoisted into the back of a homicide van. Long, brown curls had cascaded from the zippered body bag as it was tipped on one end and a white-gloved female police officer was feverishly trying to pat them back in.

Following closely behind the trolley, a young man whom I recognized as Nicky was being escorted out of the club. He looked pale and frightened. He was assisted into the back seat of a black sedan, which drove off swiftly, following the coroner's van.

Winn stepped out of the club holding Inez's arm. She leaned into his shoulder as if she were afraid of falling. Wearing a skimpy sheer outfit and shoes with straps that tied high up above her ankles, she was all legs. Gallantly, he removed his coat and draped it around her shoulders. Camera lights flashed everywhere. Winn talked to a group of persistent reporters for a minute longer and escorted "Legs" to a police car. I was surprised when he got in the driver's seat beside her and they drove off in a different direction. They looked awfully chummy. Now I was never going to find out what happened. Unless ...

I sidled up next to a film crew and approached a man about my age jotting down notes.

"I just got here, what did I miss?" I asked casually.

"Who are you?" he asked. Righfully so.

"I'm late. I missed the press release from the commanding officer. Can you fill me in?" I asked naturally, as if I did this every day.

He looked me over like I had scurvy, his eyes settling on my coat.

"Don't you think the trench coat is a little clichéd?"

"What do you expect? In case you haven't noticed, it's freezing out here. Besides it was all I had in the back of my trunk. Come on, give me a break. We could have a drink later."

The reporter leaned toward me, "Well it's not like you won't find out. A young female dancer was found dead in the club's basement locker room.

"Do you have a name?"

"First name is Maria, I'm not sure of the pronunciation of the second."

"*Dag-nol-ay*," I said, sadly sounding it out. "How did she die?"

"Strangled, and apparently with her dance costume. Funny that."

"Murder is never funny," I said starting to tremble.

"How about that drink?" he asked.

"Sure, anytime," I answered, and walked away.

Poor Maria was robbed of her moment in the spotlight. She looked so happy yesterday. I'm glad I got a chance to watch her and her partner dance. She was very beautiful. I bet she made a lot of women nervous. I remembered watching her in the meat store being followed closely around by Mr. Tony. Then I thought of Cecilia Vieira and decided I wouldn't have wanted to make her jealous.

The cards I saw chopped up at Louise's apartment meant that both women, Cecilia and Louise, knew about the false social security cards. Were all three women involved in an illegal scam and did one of them come to threaten Maria and it escalated to murder? Was Maria a loose cannon without Tony riding her all the time? I remembered how she seemed very interested in my restaurant and asked a lot of questions about my employees, even before her boss's death. Maybe she planned on going into business for herself.

There was a ready market waiting to snap up working permits in order to qualify for a legal social security number. Once you've have a number, regardless of how you received it, you don't need papers. That little white plastic card cuts out a lot of legal, time-consuming steps, especially if you're not staying in the country long. Like having a driver's licence, no one asks where you got it. It's a number, it had to be yours.

Doing the payroll for Walker's staff over the years, I've had a few employee numbers bounce out of the payroll program. Most computer programs are government-approved now and securely protected. If a card number is made up without authorization, the program won't accept it. However, it doesn't seem to care as long as the number is still in the system. Social security numbers are often borrowed and passed around between family members and their friends. In some cases, the cards might belong to holders who had left the country or were possibly dead. I have often received notices from the government, after I have filed the tax returns, stating that an employee's number was incorrect and would I send them the right one. Unfortunately, the person was usually either gone by then or had managed to legally qualify under their own name.

The employee's deductions, plus the required company contribution are remitted and at the end of February, the government fiscal year, the T4s are dutifully completed and mailed. Some are returned to sender, that's me, and others are lost in limbo. The employee deductions add up to a lot of money if you consider the thousands of unmade claims throughout the land, and I've often thought I would like to get some of it back.

Andy called out to me. When I turned to find him making his way through the crowd, I saw Louise. She looked absolutely frantic. I signalled to him to follow her and watched as his head, a mile above the rest, zipped around behind her. I knew she was gone when Andy stopped moving, spun around a few times, and began making his way back to me.

Nothing was to be achieved hanging around outside the club and since Winn was occupied, perhaps indefinitely, I wanted to get Andy to the airport before anything else happened. Although he hadn't visited my restaurant this trip, he assured me he would stop over before he returned home to Halifax after his stint in New York. I felt a little guilty for not inviting him to Walker's for a meal. Walker's Way is my pride and joy and I love showing it off. Let's face it, I haven't been myself lately and having Maria's death added to the list of murder victims was making my life miserable — something I generally left up to the staff.

It was almost eleven and Andy's flight left at midnight. The island shuttle launch was waiting the end of the pier with lights blazing. The murmuring engines released a gentle stream of bubbling water around the bilge. A damp fog, drifting over the parking pad and dock, promised to be dense on the water. Andy would feel right at home. As he was about to board he pulled me to him and kissed me on the lips. *Not bad*, I thought, but we both knew we'd be nothing more than friends.

Walker's was in shut-down mode. The waiters had reset the tables and Marlene and Marshall were balancing their cash-out. The bartender was replenishing the beer fridge and Rick was chatting to a lovely woman at the bar. I was introduced and after I said hello to everyone, made my excuses and headed upstairs. Rick followed me up to the office and I brought him up to speed on the evening's events. He wasn't nearly as callous about Maria's death as he had been about Mr. Tony's. In fact, he seemed quite concerned.

"I think you should step aside on this one, Liz. Let your friend the inspector do his job and stay out of trouble."

"Oh, if only I could, but if I can get in touch with him, I'll tell him what I suspect, and then go home to bed, all right?"

"All right, I'm leaving now." He hesitated at the door.

"Is that your date, downstairs?" I asked.

"No, a customer I met tonight, I got her number, though." He didn't seem too enthusiastic. I pulled a cockeyed face at him, hoping he'd laugh.

"I'm tired. It's been a long day without you."

"I'm sorry, Rick, I know I haven't been around much lately. You're doing a great job and I owe you."

"You owe me big, madam. Anyway, don't worry about it. I'll make sure the staff is finished their cash-out and clear the machines." He walked back toward me. "By the way, you look amazing." Then he kissed me on the cheek. Three men, three kisses, not bad for a day's work; I should wear heels more often.

As soon as Rick left I locked the door behind him and kicked off my shoes. Ahhhhh.

chapter sixteen

I dialled Winn's number and while waiting to leave a message on his machine, examined my nails. Except for a hangnail that looked good enough to eat, the rest were disgusting. I was contemplating a manicure when he surprised me by picking up on the fourth ring.

"Where are you?" he demanded instantly.

"Hello to you, too, Detective. How'd you know it was me?"

"Caller ID. Where are you?"

"I'm at the legendary Walker's Way Bistro."

"Good. Try staying there, will you?"

"Sure. Where are you?"

"I'm at Louise Kozinski's apartment. She's missing. Do you know where she is, by any chance?"

"I saw her about an hour ago outside Toscano's dance hall."

"What? Did you talk to her?"

"No. She disappeared into the crowd as soon as she saw me. I was calling to tell you that my friend and I went to her apartment and found a copy of Tony's will."

"The apartment may very well be a crime scene. You shouldn't have gone there and you shouldn't have touched anything."

"I left a message at the police station. I was frightened of not doing anything."

"I got your message. It suggested I find her butcher's apron."

"Have you got it?"

"I just finished dealing with Maria, and now I'm here. I'll get it, don't you worry."

"Don't condescend."

"Don't interfere. I needed a search warrant before I went busting into the Cheese Emporium and they take time." Winn was upset.

"I'm sorry. And I'm sorry about Maria D'Agnole. Did you find her?"

"No. A young immigration officer found her. Inez."

That information took a moment to sink in, finally I said, "Inez. Maria's friend, the dancer, she's an immigration agent."

"Yes, I told you it was police business. IMO sent her in undercover. She was inexperienced, but eager to prove herself. She fit the image better than anyone."

"She had me convinced."

"Yes, she has a French and Spanish background, she grew up dancing in tournaments like Toscano's. We were certain Maria was trafficking fake S.I.N. cards. If we caught her with a bundle, we would interrogate her to get to the source. She was to meet her early to make an exchange of false cards before the other dancers arrived."

So it wasn't about drugs, I thought. "Why would Maria trust a complete stranger?"

"She was desperate. Superior Meats was her outlet. Maria would need new connections and the cash, especially since she was unemployed and her father is dependent on her. After the girls became friendly, Inez confided that she was worried about losing her job. When she was hired at one the larger hotels downtown on the condition she had the necessary legal documents, she still didn't have a work number. She had until the end of the week, before the next payroll, to obtain one or she'd be fired.

"When it came time for her to fill out her employment record she told them she lost her wallet with all her personal information. Companies are being more careful these days. They'd probably been warned about hiring casual labour without valid documentation. They gave her three weeks to complete her personnel file, and then time was up."

"So that would appear to be a perfect excuse to be shopping for an illegal permit."

"Maria was very guarded at first, but finally confided she had a card that someone left behind when they moved back to Europe and said there probably wasn't any harm in borrowing it, you know, temporarily. She warned Inez to keep a low profile and no funny stuff. If she was caught stealing from the hotel rooms she would be put under investigation and a computer trace would reveal the card had been deactivated. Inez would be deported and denied further visitation rights to Canada. All in all, a big can of worms would be opened."

"Not to mention that Maria would lose a valuable card number."

"Yes, Inez made up a story about knowing others in the same situation. Said she knew a lot of people who wanted to know where to get instant work status even if it cost a lot. Maria was probably testing the waters with Inez at first, pretending to have only one card in her possession. Finally she confided she might be willing to help for a small fee of five hundred dollars. When she didn't show at the hall to make the exchange, Inez forced her locker open hoping she'd discover the social security cards. Instead, she found Maria stuffed inside."

"Oh my, gosh, David. That's horrible."

"I don't think she'd ever seen a dead body before. That stuff is for hardened homicide detectives like me. She's traumatized."

I paused for a moment, forcing the image out of my mind. "I told you that the apron was in the store downstairs. Why are you in Louise's apartment? Something happened in there before we arrived. Did someone report a disturbance?"

"Yes, in a manner of speaking. Mrs. Vieira called and has issued a complaint. She says Mrs. Kozinski attacked her."

"I was afraid that might happen. That's why we went over there."

"There's that 'we' again …"

"It's just a friend visiting for a couple of days, don't worry about it. I asked him to come to Louise's apartment with me because I couldn't get in touch with you. I called her before the contest to find out how she felt regarding the sale of her house to developers. Tony bought out Louise's store property in an estate sale and along with the other properties it would make a nice chunk of land to build on. Why would Cecilia go over there when she must have known how upset Louise would be about losing her family home?"

"Are you suggesting she went over there looking for trouble? Mrs. Vieira has accused Mrs. Kozinski of aggravated assault. She came down to the station in person and showed us her bruises."

"As strange as it sounds, I think Louise was expecting her visit. I don't know what took place, but the apartment was a mess and no one was there. I left everything that we found on the kitchen table for you."

"We're looking at the counterfeit cards now. I assume that was Tony Vieira's will torn up. Was that all you found?"

"Yup, and you can thank me later."

"I've notified the feds and we have a BOLO out on Louise for questioning in regards to assault and possibly murder. Do you think she killed Maria?"

"She was at Toscano's, wasn't she?"

"Do you believe an old lady like Mrs. Kozinski was responsible for all these murders, first Tony, then Albright, and now Maria? Don't forget someone was setting up your chef, as well."

"It is hard to believe, isn't it? But don't be fooled by Louise Kozinski's appearance. She's not that old, and hey … wait a minute. You just said Daniel was set up. Does that mean you think he and his sister are innocent?"

"Daniel's apron tested clean, so I've released them both. I could charge Meriel with lying to the police, but I probably won't pursue it."

"Thanks, Winn." He turned that around fast. Now I was thanking him.

"You're welcome. Now let me finish my job."

I had no sooner laid down the phone when it rang again. I was shocked to hear the voice on the other end.

"Liz, you've got to help me."

Doesn't anybody say hello anymore? "Louise?"

"Tony's wife is going to kill me for the deed to my building."

"That's a very serious accusation," I said.

"It's true. Tony left me the store in his will. It reverted back to my ownership if he died."

"You should talk to the police, they're looking for you."

"That cop, the one we met in my store the day after Tony was killed? He likes you. I could tell the way he looked at you. And he came to your rescue that night in the alley when those thugs came after you. Talk to him for me."

I wondered how she knew about the intended mugging, but word spread fast around the market. Unless there was another reason, like she witnessed the whole thing from her upstairs window and didn't want to get involved, or on the contrary, hoped I'd be killed.

"Why would he leave you the store, Louise? It seems strange to me with his wife still alive. I assumed his wife would stand to inherit it all."

"So did I. Imagine my surprise when I saw the will. I was sleeping with her husband for the last five years. I think she knew about our affair, but pretended not to care. Cecilia was all about appearances. She was only interested in his money, not making love to a butcher."

"But you were, Louise?"

"I wasn't at first. He dangled the forfeited mortgage over my head. If I slept with him he would go easy on the rent. At first I went along with it because I had nowhere else to go. I was so lonely for company after my husband died and I grew to like his attention. He wasn't all bad. I never went hungry. And we were the same age and could talk about old times. I made him feel like a man. She didn't. She belittled him, made fun of the way the girls called him Mr. Tony. Said it was undignified for a businessman. Tony came over last week and said if anything ever happened to him, I would get my property back. He left it to me in the will. I never dreamed he was telling the truth. When I saw her at the door I was afraid to let her in, but she insisted."

"So, did you have a nice visit?" She didn't know I'd already been to her apartment and seen the state of the place.

"It started off that way. Then she accused me of knowing about the conditions of the will all along, that I talked Tony into it and then murdered him to get the property back. She offered me a cash settlement if I moved out and I told her I would never give her the satisfaction. She got very angry and started yelling at me. I ran down the stairs and left her in the apartment."

"You left her behind."

"Yes, I had to. I was frightened. I still am."

"Why did you go to the dance?"

"I wanted to talk to Maria. Tony said Maria knew everything."

"About what, those cards we found at your place? Were you in on it?"

"What cards?" She issued a loud audible sigh and said, "I never know what anyone's talking about anymore and I never got a chance to talk to Maria. She was already dead."

chapter seventeen

I closed the office door behind me, whistled nonchalantly past a couple of ghouls loitering under the exit sign, and then bolted down the stairs into the restaurant. I had mixed feelings about Louise. She said she was on her way back home and I agreed to meet her there before Winn and his posse could take her in for questioning.

It was only midnight, but everyone had gone. Years ago, when smoking was permitted, we often stayed open until one or two in the morning. Drink orders flew from the bar, one more drink, one more cigarette, one more cigarette, one more drink. No one wanted to leave. The waiters were kept busy lighting cigarettes, exchanging brimming ashtrays, and providing endless change for the cigarette machine downstairs. At closing time, stubborn customers had to be pried from the booths, and the waiters were often forced to don their coats and turn off all the lights before the squatters took the hint.

Rick left one night, pretending to lock the customers in by mistake. He went back ten minutes later, just as they were pressing their faces against the glass, trying to catch a lone passerby's attention. Ah, the good ol' smoking days. As a business person, the loss of income was bad; as a health-conscious mother, I dealt with it.

I checked that the tables were set up for tomorrow, the bar wiped down, and the beer fridge restocked. I tried the front door. It was secure, the door alarm set.

The kitchen was empty, too. The pots and pans had been washed and put away, the floors mopped, and the stainless-steel counters sprayed with disinfectant. Rick would make sure the refrigerator doors were closed, the gas knobs were turned off tightly on the Garlands, and the lids on the flour and sugar bins were secure. I saw that the push-bar on the back door was chained and the side window's cage was locked in place. I was ready to leave.

Just as I was walking back toward the front dining room, past the stairwell, I heard a loud crash come from the basement.

I hollered from the top of the stairs, "Rick is that you? What are you doing down there?"

Kitty answered with a loud mew.

Darn. It sounded like glass. She must have knocked something off a shelf. I should clean it up before she stepped in it or insects and other various vermin were attracted to the contents. While I was down there I'd have a look at the new tail Rick said she had acquired. The growing collection of animal tails had begun to weigh on my mind.

The stairs led down into a vestibule where the public washrooms were located. EMPLOYEES ONLY marked a door that opened into the basement. Two of the foundation walls in the small lobby were the original limestone rock. The wall had suffered little from the flood, but the drywall surrounding the bathrooms had dissolved and had to be completely rebuilt. After it took two cement trucks to fill in the gaping hole where the water main had broken under the street and terrified our dishwasher, Abdul. The professional opinion of the building inspector was the foundation would still be standing for another hundred years.

When I first took over the restoration of the restaurant I decided to leave the stone walls exposed. I'm glad I did.

Rick's briefcase was sitting outside the men's washroom door, indicating he hadn't left after all. The tail could wait another day. Louise was waiting at home for me.

"Rick, are you in the washroom? I thought I heard you down here. I think Kitty broke something, but if you've got it covered I'm going to leave, okay?"

He didn't answer. I pushed the bathroom door open a little. Immediately, I was overwhelmed by the smell.

"Rick?"

I knew he wasn't in there; I couldn't see his feet under the stall door. I pushed the door open the rest of the way and stepped inside, holding my nose. The urinal drain was plugged by one of the melted deodorant pucks, leaving an inch of yellow liquid pooling in its porcelain bowl. I would have to remind myself to fish out the shrunken slivers from the drain tomorrow. Someday I'll make a reality video and send it to all the naive students in schools around the world seeking glamour and fortune in the hospitality business.

I opened the basement fire door. I couldn't see anything broken and decided I was probably mistaken about the source of the crash. The hundred-year-old pipes rattled and pinged, the ancient wooden beams creaked, echoing throughout the building.

After the flood receded, and I mean that quite literally, the ground had absorbed so much water that three feet of silt and slimy mud was left behind. The smell of oil permeated the spot where the two furnace tanks had been ripped out and smashed against one another. Except for the eight-by-ten, room-sized refrigerator, everything had to be rebuilt or replaced. We had to disinfect the walk-in and the compressor was replaced, but the unit was solidly built and had withstood the flood. Everything else was ruined. Hard to believe water damage is so irreparable. Water covers everything, seeping into the smallest crevice.

"Hey Rick, are you in here?" I heard a muffled sound. I went in and stood quietly. I spotted a broken mason jar on the floor. A few old rusty nails had spilled out and I picked them up one by one in case Kitty stepped on one. A wrench was leaning against the wall. It looked like it belonged to Bill, our young, tattooed repairman. He probably dropped it last week when he fixed the compressor and didn't notice. I put it on the shelf beside the nails.

Two brand-new gas furnaces at the far end of the basement kept the upstairs tenants warmer last winter, but in the process burned over a thousand dollars of fuel a month. Kitty had made a cozy hideaway behind one of the new furnaces and I decided to head for her box of tails. I bent down a little to get a better look. The lights went out. The box quickly disappeared as did everything else, including my hands, which I was holding up in front of me to see how dark it was. It was bloody dark. And I wasn't alone. Someone was in the basement with me. I was getting tired of this. If Rick jumped out and scared me, I was going to kill him.

"Cut it out, Rick. Rick? Is that you?" Whether he scared me or not, I really hoped it was.

"Hello, my friend."

"Louise?"

"Can I get you anything, my friend, perhaps another free sample?"

I could barely hear her. Her voice was raspy, almost a whisper.

"Is that you, Louise? It doesn't sound like you. I thought we agreed to meet at your apartment."

"I changed my mind."

"You wanted my help? I promise to put in a good word for you with the police."

"It's too late for that."

"Don't try anything funny, I know kung fu."

I heard a muffled laugh. I would have laughed along with her, but was afraid of peeing myself. She was slowly moving closer. She would have to be careful in the dark. The dark, it was the one thing that might save me.

A tiny rebuilt staff washroom with a separate change room attached, where the kitchen people could change into their whites, was on my right. A floor-to-ceiling shelving unit holding all manner of linen and shelves containing dried goods was on my left. Paper supplies were stacked in cartons beside a small collection of lumber remnants, and pails of industrial cleaners and cans of paint resided in one corner. I could find my out blindfolded. I've had the lights turned off on me so many times either as a joke or by mistake that I'm used to the dark. I admit I broke a toe trying to find my way out of the staff washroom one night after Manuel, thinking everyone had left, had turned out the lights. He said he never heard such obscenities and knew it was me. "How flattering," I told him. The point was that I've had to feel my way from one end to the other of the debris-filled cellar numerous times.

The only difference this time was the exit sign over the door was out, too. The fire code requires the sign to be on a separate circuit in case there is an emergency. That meant Louise had planned this meeting ahead of time. She could have slipped in here during a busy lunch-hour rush and no one would have noticed. We don't lock the door to the basement anymore. Rick and I have had to remove the door from its hinges so many times after someone inadvertently locked and lost the key that we thought it was in our best interest to remove the lock altogether. Consequently, we told no one to leave any valuables down here. Even shoes are brought upstairs and hidden behind the bar. Thieves steal shoes if there's nothing else to take, especially expensive athletic shoes. Easy, pull the old ones off, put the new ones on, and walk out.

"I knew it was you Louise. I told Detective Winn how I figured it out."

"I'm sure you did. Too bad your boyfriend is going to find your body when he gets here."

"Why kill me? I didn't do anything. I like you. I thought we were friends." I was stalling for time, slowly moving toward the corner where we kept bits of lumber. I was hoping to find something with which to protect myself.

"Stop moving. I'm going to find you, I've just been playing. I found a flashlight upstairs in your kitchen. Handy, I never thought of bringing one along myself."

She turned on the flashlight and aimed it directly in my face. I felt like a deer trapped in the headlights.

"I'm going to tell you a little story and then I have to go. I was that sick bastard's whore long before his pretty new wife came along. Tony dangled the mortgage over my head, telling me as long as I slept with him I could keep the store for a reduced rent. My own father's store, can you believe that bastard?"

"But you said you grew to like him."

"Shut up. When the bank foreclosed on the mortgage after my father died, and my husband became ill, they let him have it. I almost died of shame. I thought of moving, but where would I go? I'm fifty-seven now. After my husband passed away, I was alone. My friends are the market sellers. I've lived over the store my whole life."

"Of course, if Tony sold his properties for condos, then you would be forced to leave."

"Correct. The councillor turned out to be as evil as him, bringing in rats and protecting the crackheads' legal right to squat. What about my rights? Two of a kind, they were. Have you ever heard of the saying, 'Dogs smell their own dirt'? Well, they were rolling in it. They deserved to die."

I thought she laughed again, but quickly realized she was wheezing. Then, in a croaking whisper, which was getting creepier by the second, she continued, "The market needed revitalization. It can work, but they both saw to it that didn't happen. I taught them a lesson."

"Tony bequeathed you the store. Now you own it again. Don't make this worse."

"Too late, I told you."

"What about Maria? How did she figure in?"

"Missy got too greedy. She was blackmailing me for a bigger cut of the profit and getting sloppy. I needed that money to fund my own land-buying scheme."

I listened, thinking that Louise must suffer from multiple-personality disorder. She was extremely agitated and losing focus because of it — I hoped. The light from the flashlight was wavering. I had to make a move while she was rambling.

"I provide a necessary service to immigrants. Without a card how can they work? I should have realized that Inez woman was an investigating immigration officer, but I've been little preoccupied with losing my store. I saw her poking around the market a few times in the last few months and recognized her at the dance club one night while I was watching Maria. My whole operation would have been discovered and shut down soon."

"I'm not part of any of this, why come after me? I'm on your side."

"You know too much and you keep getting involved. I thought I'd hit you hard enough and by the time you were discovered in the Dumpster, you would have bled to death or wound up in a coma. I should have cut you up like I did Tony, only there wasn't time. I've been trying to frame your chef, but you keep interrupting my best efforts."

I slid my foot along the ground behind me and took a step.

She was moving swiftly toward me. "That's enough chatter."

The light was blinding me. I tried backing up farther, and stumbled over a box, throwing me off balance. Instantly, she pushed me to the ground and scrambled on top, straddling my chest. I couldn't get my breath. Then she started hitting me with the flashlight as hard as she could. I was waving my arms around, deflecting the blows, when one landed on the back of my head on the same tender spot I was hurt before. A trickle of wet ran down my shirt. I was losing consciousness fast, but with every ounce of strength left in my body, I kicked out one last time, jolting the flashlight out of her hand. I rolled across the cement floor, grabbed the flashlight and pointed it directly in her face. That's when I blacked out.

I touched my scalp gingerly. My fingers made contact with a circle of crusty blood that had congealed around the base of a throbbing lump of flesh. My new wound was perched on top of the old wound and it ached mercilessly. I brought my hand down to my face to check for blood. I couldn't see any, of course, because I couldn't see my hand. It was still pitch black. Apparently my brain couldn't keep up with the situation.

Wherever I was, it was freezing. I heard a moan behind me, sending goosebumps along my arms. I sat up straight and felt a cold, wooden floor under me, then heard another moan. I got up on my knees and brushed against a cardboard box. Feeling inside, I touched tall, waxy cartons. They were cold, too. I crawled ahead a couple of feet and touched something soft. My hands groped about until I realized it was a pair of legs.

"Welcome."

"Rick!" I squealed.

"Liz!"

I sat down beside him. "What are you doing in here?"

"Where are we?"

"The basement walk-in."

"If I'd known, I would have sprung for a room. Ow!"

"Rick, are you hurt?" My eyes were adjusting to a faint glimmer of light. I helped him to sit upright, propping him against one of the lower shelves.

"My head aches worse than a gin hangover. I can't seem to move my arm either."

"Is it broken?" I asked.

"Maybe, but before I die, tell me what we're doing in here."

"There's a mad person out there trying to kill me."

"Who's mad?"

"Never mind, it's a long story. I thought you left for home until I saw your briefcase outside the men's toilet. What were you doing down here?"

"I decided to unclog the men's urinal before I left. I needed to get a screwdriver from the basement, but when I opened the door, the lights were all out, including the emergency exit light. The way our luck's been going, I thought I better put a new bulb in before we got a fire inspection. I was standing on the ladder when someone knocked it over and attacked me from behind." Rick's head nodded against my shoulder for a moment. He mumbled, "Did you try the door?"

Why didn't I think of that? I almost slapped my head, but remembered it had taken enough punishment for one day. There was enough room in between the dairy shelves for me to stand up. A narrow aisle ran down the centre of the fridge, and feeling my way slowly toward the thick metal door, I found the safety handle and pushed it down hard. That should have popped the door open, but it didn't. My worst nightmare was coming true: claustrophobia being at the top of my list of fears.

Rick sounded worried. "I hope we're not going to be in here for the night." His face was so pale I could see it in the dark. I wasn't faring much better. My head was killing me. Then I realized I could see shadows and make out dim shapes around us. There had to be light coming in from somewhere.

I sniffed the air, recognizing the smell of burning wood. A thin wisp of smoke curled under the massive fridge door. My senses went on red alert. The pungent smell of gasoline fumes reached me first and then I could hear crackling. The basement was on fire. The walk-in was sealed tightly with insulation and sheet-metal walls, but it wouldn't keep out the smoke for long. Why wasn't the fire alarm going off? Then I heard it ringing faintly upstairs.

It was no longer cold inside the fridge; the air was rapidly changing.

"Thanks, Liz. I'm getting warmer now," Rick said and then sighed deeply.

I put my ear to the door and thought I heard a faint meow.

"Kitty…?" I called. Was she trapped in the fire? Oh, no, I couldn't bear the thought. Then I heard her meow again. I followed the sound to the back of the cooler, stepping carefully over Rick's slumped body. "Kitty, where are you?"

She stuck her head out from around an apple crate and I swear she smiled. Maybe it was the smoke. I tore away the boxes stacked against the wall, exposing a hole the size of a cantaloupe. I had found her secret passage way. Getting down on my stomach, I turned my head on its side and pressed my eye against it. There was light and the air was fresh. I sucked in a lung full, and, getting my senses back, realized I was looking into the candy store's basement attached to us next door.

Last year's flood had caused major damage to the room-sized walk-in, after all. The metal liner didn't run along the back of the fridge where it was attached to the adjoining brick wall. A foam sheath remained in place, but it was dank and its wooden frame was rotting at the floor boards.

I could feel the heat on the other three walls. Butter was melting inside its foil wrap and dripping onto a case of eggs below. The air inside the fridge was getting thicker. Positioning Rick's head by the opening, I lay beside him on the floor. Kitty had disappeared again. I put my hand through the hole and starting yelling for help, the candy store had been closed for hours, but it was better than thinking about being burned alive.

My throat was soon raw from yelling and the heat was suffocating. I was nodding off, perhaps for all eternity, when something fell on top of me, startling me awake. A two-foot piece of insulation running along the back wall had broken off. My arm flew up, knocking another piece loose. It was soft with mildew. I remembered Bill saying something about the liner of the fridge being compromised by the flood. He warned me that I was going to have to replace the walk-in compressor again if I didn't seal the leak. I wasn't a big fan of closed spaces and never investigated. If I had, my nose would have discovered this amount of moldering dampness long ago.

I sat up and turned around so my feet were facing the wall. With all my might, I kicked at the base of the wet wall. Another large section of the insulation fell apart, landing on my head. It was like sponge. I knocked out the wooden slats it had been attached to, leaving the brick wall exposed between the two basements. A few of the bricks were white from moldy decay. I kicked again, knocking two bricks into the candy store's cellar, and then sent two more flying. The remaining brick was solid and I was losing my breath from the exertion.

I now had a hole big enough for me to shove my head and neck through and breathed in, gulping down the intoxicating, fresh air. I could see Kitty calmly licking herself on the other side. Rick coughed. I pulled my head back in and nudged his head into the hole. I turned around and saw flames licking at the base of the fridge door. When I poured a carton of milk along the crack it sizzled. I started dumping everything I could get my hands on, orange juice, Clamato juice, Vichyssoise, anything wet. Wonder of wonders, I found a case of mineral water. It was warm, but I drank heavily and poured some over my head. Rick coughed again.

"I must have died and gone to your heaven by mistake," he said, "look at all the chocolate bars." I pulled his head back into the fridge. I gave him a drink and poured water over his clothes. We took turns poking our heads through the hole while screaming for help.

"Break the wall down. Hurry they'll burn to death."

I recognized Winn's voice instantly, and then heard heavy boots clomping down the basement stairs of the candy store. I poked my head through, "David, quick, Rick's hurt and the fire is coming inside."

"Get back, Liz! We're breaking the wall down."

Firemen pulled Rick and I through the broken wall to the candy store just as a loud crack split the air and flames engulfed the floor behind us. I looked around to see if the seat of my pants was on fire.

chapter eighteen

Rick was whisked away in the back of a waiting ambulance while I dangled my feet from the back of an emergency van with an oxygen mask over my face. By the time they dragged me out of the candy store I looked like a melted ice-cream cone. My entire body was thick with the dairy products I had poured over myself to keep cool. A clump of yogurt had dried in my hair and grease from a ten-pound block of butter had covered my clothes. Rick was in the same condition, but he was gone. He didn't have to suffer the sidelong glances and double takes of the calendar-worthy firemen.

Winn stood a few feet away, quietly talking to the fire marshal. As soon as I was pulled free from the hole in the wall, David lifted me in his arms and carried me up the stairs to safety. His long, grey coat was smeared with creamy bits of food. I couldn't begin to describe how happy I was to see him, at least not without making myself cry.

The chief was providing details about the fire. He turned around, speaking loudly enough now for me to hear. "The paper supplies were doused with a quick accelerant. The loose lumber, paint cans, and stored grease containers would have enabled the fire to spread quickly. I suggest, Ms. Walker, that you store these items separately in the future."

I was about to protest that the basement was greatly needed storage space, but he held up a gloved hand to silence me. As if clairvoyant, he said, "Find another place or I'll be back one of these days to make sure you do. Luckily, the fire was contained in the basement due to the heavy fire door that separates the private area from the public washrooms. There was absolutely no damage to the restaurant." Next time that steel door bangs shut on my heel I promised not to swear like a stevedore.

The fireman explained that if the walk-in refrigerator had been solid at the back, Rick and I would have died from smoke inhalation and burned to a crisp. He didn't actually say burned to a crisp, but I added that for him.

The fire was almost out. There was so much stuff kept down there it had taken them some time to thoroughly search through the debris for live embers. The marshal's walkie-talkie rattled and a voice came through loud and clear.

"We found something, sir. I think you might want to have a look."

Both men disappeared into the restaurant. I took the mask off; my head had cleared from the pure oxygen and reality was settling in. How long was I going to have to remain closed for business this time? I started to tally the damage when two firemen carrying a loaded stretcher emerged onto the sidewalk. Winn followed closely behind. Seeing my look of shock, he came to my side.

"That's Arthur Tilson isn't it?" I said, flabbergasted. Winn nodded his head.

"Probably. It's a little hard to tell right now. But we believe he was the guy who attacked you. He was found unconscious in the staff washroom. It was a small, closed room; the fumes must have overcome him. We found a charred flashlight lodged behind the toilet, a wig, and a pair of glasses in the toilet bowl. If he dropped the flashlight and then dropped his glasses, he may have become confused and panicked. We also found this." Winn handed me a partially melted tape recorder, the tape inside a liquid mass. "You'll have to testify in court that he tried to murder you and Rick. It won't be for a while though, and that is, if he recovers. He's badly burned. He was trying to tell us something but we didn't get it."

I jumped off the back of the ambulance. The oxygen mask sprung off my face and hit the sidewalk. I barely noticed. "What is wrong with me?" Both men shook their heads in unison.

"You know, Winn, I can't believe Tilson had it in him to stage all these murders, let alone execute them, and try to blame them on Louise! He was a bit of a wet noodle, if you know what I mean. Now that I think about it, I remember hearing that same hoarse voice arguing at the C.N.E. I was never sure that it was Daniel in the hallway. I remember the rasp clearly now. At the community meeting Tilson seemed fine. But I noticed after he announced that Tony's wife was selling the business and everyone started yelling that his voice got high-pitched and reedy. Some kind of a nervous condition, possibly. It was his voice I heard yelling before I had my head shoved into the water fountain. I should have known he was involved."

"Why would you?" Winn answered. "You left me a message warning me to suspect Louise Kozinski. I have to admit I thought it was Meriel and Daniel Chapin right up to tonight. It was only after the apron I found in your office tested clean that I revised my opinion. I was beginning to believe it had to be Louise, too. But just because Tilson was pretending to be her doesn't mean she wasn't initially involved. He could have been partnering with her and then decided to set her up."

"Why would he go to all the trouble of pretending to be her if he intended on killing me?"

"I think he intended to leave a tape of your conversation in the basement, pointing a finger at Louise. Possibly he thought the tape would be safe in the staff washroom, but the fire got out of hand. Arson is a science in itself. He's lucky we got to him when we did."

My son pulled up to the curb in my car, which he had fetched from the parking lot. Winn handed me my purse.

"It was upstairs on the bar where you left it. I found your keys in it."

Jon came around and opened the door for me. With a promise that I would see my doctor tomorrow, I wiggled out of going to the hospital for a check-up. I felt fine. I just needed a shower and a good night's sleep.

I rolled down the window. Winn leaned on the door.

"Take your mother home, young man, and make her stay there. And keep an eye on her for concussion."

"I'm telling you, Arthur Tilson wasn't alone in this," I said. "He had to be working with Tony's wife. Cecilia is the mastermind. I'm convinced."

Jon suddenly spoke up, "Did you say Cecilia? That's a familiar name. I saw it yesterday on several purchases of property that you asked me to look up. Only the last name was Santos. Cecilia Santos."

I looked at Winn. "You better find them before before it's too late."

"Don't worry. I've got both of them in jail."

Before I could get another word out, Jon stepped on the gas. The sun was starting to come up.

chapter nineteen

I slept until two in the afternoon. I needed to, considering Jon was waking me up every two hours to make sure I hadn't gone into a coma. I finally woke up for good to the alarm and the phone ringing simultaneously. Winn was on his way over to my house to give me a lift to the doctor's. I told him it wasn't necessary, but delighted when he insisted. I'm sure Jon would be thrilled that I could be properly ruled out for head trauma, as well.

An hour later, Winn was waiting out front in a dark blue unmarked sedan. I ran outside rather than make him come up to the house. It wasn't a date. Even so, I tried on ten different outfits until I was satisfied.

"You look good," Winn volunteered as I climbed in the front seat.

"I didn't want to scare the doctor."

"Well you scare me, but it's not because you look good."

"That's rather ambiguous."

"Let's talk about you and me later."

Winn pulled down the street and headed for Toronto General Hospital on University Avenue. Since my doctor was leaving for a medical convention in Calgary the next day, he arranged for me to come to a cubbyhole of an office he used to interview surgery patients. Winn drove slowly. "I have some bad news," he said.

"Arthur Tilson died?"

"No, he's conscious, at least enough to get us a warrant for Cecilia Vieira's arrest. Unfortunately, we can't find her."

"You said you had her in jail last night, I mean this morning."

"Her lawyer got her out on bail."

Without covering his mouth, he opened wide and yawned.

"Have you been to sleep yet, David?" It was my turn to say how awful he looked, but uncharacteristically I held it back.

"Too busy to sleep. After Mrs. Vieira made the complaint about Mrs. Kozinski attacking her, I decided to bring both of them in for questioning. Especially since Kosinzski claimed it was the other way around. She charged that Cecilia Vieira came to her apartment, threatened, and then attacked her there. I needed time to interview them separately in order to validate their stories."

"I was more concerned for Cecilia's safety than anything. Boy was I wrong."

"Listen Liz, it was a toss-up right from the beginning. Don't feel too bad, you led us to Louise. When we brought her in, she bawled liked a baby. Not Cecilia Vieira, though. She didn't shed a tear, in fact she was defiant with an unmistakable air of superiority hard at work. Most criminals are egoists and she was no exception."

"What time was this?"

"After our phone conversation last night, you said you saw Louise in the crowd of spectators outside

Toscano's. I radioed down with a description to pick her up and they found her wandering around in a daze. In the meantime, I found Mrs. Vieira at home. She wasn't too happy about being interrupted. It looked like she was celebrating with a magnum of champagne in her hand when she came to the door. The one question that constantly nagged me was why she never got very sick after ingesting the rat poison."

"I know what you mean. I thought it was very lucky she didn't like red meat. It saved her from a fatal overdose."

"Luck or a calculated mistake to make her look innocent. After the hospital pumped out her stomach, they found no trace of the poison the contents. We knew she vomited before the ambulance arrived, but it was cleaned up by the convention staff immediately along with the councillor's vomit. Forensics went through the stomach contents, but at the time no one thought it was murder. It was just assumed to be a lethal case of food poisoning. Her bite of meat may have had only a little in it, but it didn't make sense.

"I shuffled through my desk for a picture of the sit-down dinner taken by a newspaper reporter. The picture showed a close-up of Mrs. Vieira with Albright sitting close beside her. She was holding up her fork with a piece of steak on the end of it, supposedly from his plate. It didn't show her actually eating it," Winn said, thoughtfully.

"Could someone have doctored the food after she was photographed sharing the councillor's breakfast — a waiter or another guest?" I asked.

"Could have, but we questioned everyone and found no connections whatsoever. I wondered about the recent changes to Tony's will. The notarized date on the new will showed that it had been changed a week ago. Right before Tony was murdered. Louise claimed that she didn't have any knowledge of the bequest until two days ago. Cecilia says that Louise knew all along. There was one other person I needed to question concerning the will."

"Who?" How many more players were going to star in this twisted production?

"Vieira's estate lawyer. He just got back from Portugal. I spoke with him this morning. Mr. Vieira apparently came to his office last week in a total frenzy and asked that his will be changed. In the event that anything happen to him all his properties would be left to Louise Kozinski."

"Could he do that?"

"Not according to the lawyer. That is to say, not on the properties he purchased with his wife's name on the deeds, but the cheese shop was his alone."

"He knew the deal on the condos would go south without Louise's place. Was it just out of spite he changed the will or a safety rope in case he suspected his wife of double dealing? He would want to sell the properties as soon as possible if that were the case. Maybe he thought she was going to divorce him and hook up with Albright. She'd still need that property and she couldn't get her hands on it without him. She'd have to stay married to him."

"In other words, he never intended for Louise to inherit her father's store back. So much for their romantic involvement. She actually liked the guy."

"Too bad she trusted him. Sounds like a case of Stockholm syndrome — she fell in love with her captor."

"I'm glad you said that and not me," Winn remarked. "In reality, he was unwittingly setting the stage for his own death, and supplying Louise with motive for murder. Cecilia must have believed he was serious about the will and she was angry about the double-cross. It's even possible he threatened her with divorce when he found out about her affair, and knowing it might take years of probate to iron it all out, Cecilia took a short-cut. She would still inherit the other properties."

"And she would still make a lot of money even with separate townhouses built on the site."

"What your son said last night sunk in after about twenty coffees," said Winn. "After Cecilia disappeared this morning, I ran a background on her to get the address where she was born. I was hoping I could track down family or old friends. Lo and behold, the security card she used for ID belonged to a 'Cecilia Santos,' who has been dead for twenty years."

"She was building her own empire. Where did she get the money to buy the other real estate?"

"Now this is a big leap, but we think Cecilia ran the operation on her own and Tony, well, either he didn't care, or he didn't know. Probably didn't know, he really was just the butcher man after all."

"Last question, why kill Albright?"

"Possibly the same reason she killed her husband. She didn't want to share. The councillor probably assumed that with Tony gone, he would become heir to his throne."

"There's still Maria's murder," I pointed out.

"That's easy," said Winn. Boy, he could be cocky when he wanted to be. "She killed Maria to shut her up about the card scam. Without Maria's testimony, IMO can't confirm the source of origin. And perhaps Maria didn't even know. We thought Anthony and Cecilia Vieira ran the operation at ground level, now we think it was all Cecilia's doing. As to how high up the conspiracy goes, we'll have to investigate further to find out. I'm afraid our agent 'Inez' won't want to be involved this time."

"Inez is lovely," I said looking out the passenger window.

I felt Winn's eyes on me. "What's that got to do with anything?"

I shrugged my shoulders and continued to stare out the window.

Winn continued, "Between conscious and unconscious states, Arthur Tilson provided us with enough of a statement to issue a warrant to search the Vieira house. We discovered concentrated rat poison in a perfume bottle in Cecilia's medicine cabinet and when we jacked open the wall safe, we found a gold plastic bag containing a knife wrapped in a torn safety apron and a protective chain-mail vest. The DNA lab will have the evidence back tomorrow, but I didn't need it to arrest her."

"Maria carried her costume in a gold bag. A trophy for Cecilia, perhaps?"

"Until we find her, we'll have to wait to ask. She was gone from the house by the time we did the search.

"Is Louise still locked up?"

"We let her go after she gave us her personal history on Mrs. Vieira's background. Apparently when Cecilia first arrived in Toronto, she applied for a job at the Cheese Emporium. She had a certificate in Deli Management from Lisbon, which qualified her to be a skilled butcher of smoked meats and fish. Louise wanted to hire her, but she couldn't afford to, despite the fact that she would have been good for a faltering business. She was quite beautiful and young and despite the gravelly timbre to her voice, quite charming. Louise sent her along to Quality Meats, knowing that Tony would hire her. He did, and a year later wedding bells rang."

"What about Tilson? If he lives, what are you going to charge him with?"

"I think that accessory to murder, conspiracy to murder, and attempted murder should cover it."

"You said you talked to him, what did he tell you?"

"He said to tell you he was sorry. His conscience made him save you once, but he couldn't do it again or else the love of his life would leave him."

"He was the one who called the police about me in the Dumpster?

"Yup, poor dupe."

"Hey, he tried to kill me."

"Love is blind. I didn't have the heart to tell him she disappeared."

"Cecilia probably initiated the affair with Arthur Tilson. Unlikely too many women like her would give him the time of day."

"He had no idea who he was dealing with. He was way out of his league. By the time Mrs. Vieira convinced him to help her; she had already administered a fatal dose of poison to Albright and chopped up her husband. And that was just for starters."

"If you weren't such a buttinski, she wouldn't have bothered with you. She planned all along to frame Tilson for the poisoning and Louise for Mr. Tony's and Maria's murders. She would be a very rich lady if it weren't for you."

"Do you think she'll come after me?"

"We'll find her before that happens. She has nowhere to go. I've got men placed outside Superior Meats and her home. We found a great deal of cash in the store safe. I surprised her at her home, so I doubt she has much money. We're waiting for her to show." He looked over at me. "Don't worry, she'll be lucky to get out of prison before she's ninety."

I was thinking the prospect over when Winn's cell rang and he answered quickly, "Winn here. Yes, yes, all right, don't do anything. I'm five minutes away, thanks."

He reached under his seat and pulled out a plastic portable emergency light. Arm through the window, he placed it on the roof and a second later, the rotating red flash lit up the car.

"Remember Nathan, the homeless guy? He just spotted Cecilia in the alley. He followed her to Superior

Meats, but when she saw the police she bolted. He lost track of her, but she's around, I'm sure."

We were on University, speeding along side streets and reached the market in under five. Winn turned into the alley behind the meat store. He turned off the flashing light and coasted along quietly. He passed the uniforms standing outside the back door and motioned to them. They shook their heads.

"She's hiding here somewhere and needs money. She can't get into the store, where could she be?" I looked along the alley. The rear doors to all the stores were shut tight. Most of them had security alarm doors that didn't even have handles on the outside, only locks for specifically made keys.

Then I remembered that there was one place that left the back door open. Air conditioning was out of the question with the large ovens going all the time. Even in winter, a door or window was always left open to allow a draft.

"Try the bakery," I said. "It's near the end of the alley."

Sure enough, the door was open. Winn silently pulled the cruiser in behind the store.

"Wait here."

"No, I'm coming with you."

"Shit."

I stopped at the doorway, allowing Winn to get ahead of me. A dark man, arms speckled with flour and lost, deep in private thought, was slowly rolling around a clump of dough on a heavy wooden table. He barely looked up when Winn showed him his badge. At this time of day, he was the only baker in the kitchen. The other areas, nearer the ovens, cleaned and ready to go, would be filled later with bustling activity throughout the wee hours of the night.

The air was close, scented with cinnamon and chocolate, and the rhythmic kneading motion of his hands, over and under, tuck, over, and under, tuck, were lulling me to sleep. Winn had disappeared into the front of the store and was showing the clerk a photo. I watched the man with the quiet face until I thought I was going to faint. I couldn't really sit down without getting flour all over my clothes and decided to go back outside. The fresh air revived me, and, standing by a small barred window set into the back wall, I watched for Winn to come back.

I looked at the large bags of flour standing loosely about the room and noticed a large mound of flour spilled in one corner. I wondered how they dealt with the health department. It would be impossible to keep the floors clean. I looked again. There were handprints on the floor outlined in the spilt flour. One of the bags moved.

Frozen, I watched Winn walk into the room. The bag fell over with a heavy thud and flour showered the air. Cecilia Vieira shoved it out of the way and, jumping from behind it, dove at Winn's legs. He was thrown off balance and teetered. Then he slipped in the flour and slammed to the ground onto his back. Cecilia bent over, lifting a knife high in the air, ready to plunge. I ran through the door, the baker whistled shrilly, and tossed me a rolling pin the size of a baseball bat. I caught it and yelled, "Hey, Cecilia, want a chocolate?"

She twisted around and screamed, "You stupid, interfering bitch!" Then she lunged.

I swung the bat and landed it squarely on the top of her head. Cecilia folded onto her knees and collapsed. The baker threw his hands in the air and hollered,

"She's out!"

THE END

(Well, not quite.)

epilogue

The good news is that my son Jon and Susan, the police rookie, are engaged. I have their assurances they will both finish their degrees and live together for a year before planning a wedding.

The bad news is that I've been stood up. Winn was supposed to pick me up at Walker's Way twenty minutes ago, except he called and said he wasn't coming. His wife got wind of the fact he was interested in another woman and has apparently reconsidered her position. If nothing else, he said he had to talk it over with her and he owed it to her. I understood didn't I? Of course I understood. There's a picture of me in the dictionary beside the word.

In the meantime, it wasn't all bad. The restaurant was packed, the customers were swooning over Daniel's food, and Rick, one arm in a cast, was dazzling a bevy of teachers and looking as if he just won the lottery. I had a bowl of cognac in front of me soon to be consumed and was contentedly watching the happy customers while jazz murmured softly in the background and the cat was playing with a ...

CHEQUE, PLEASE!

glossary

Bag of Bones	A bag of fresh bones from the butcher used to make a concentrated stock base
Bag of white	A ten-pound quantity of chicken breast with the bone out
Bar Back	Open bottles of house wines or liquor. Can also refer to second bartender in command
BOLO	A police alert meaning "Be on the Lookout"
Bucket of Death	A pail of water with a miniature tilting gang plank
Comp.	A free drink or food bought by the house. (establishment)
Covers	Number of meals served to customers in a given period

Deck	On deck, referring to food orders waiting in sequence to be filled by the chef
Demi glace	A base made from veal bones
El dente	Translated literally means "to the tooth," (not cooked to mush!)
Expediter	Person who controls pick-up and delivery of plated foods
Garland	A common brand of commercial oven used primarily in restaurants
Hobart	Large upright floor model dough mixer
"In the weeds"	When the chef has more orders than he can handle
Plated	Prepared meal waiting to be served
Prima vera	Pasta mixed with vegetables. A vegetarian alternative on most menus
Rail	A trough containing easy access bottles of the most common house-brand liquor
Reach-in	Refrigerator you reach into with your hands. Side by side, with two full length doors that open out in the middle
Salamander	A broiler attached to the top of a stove range used to heat flash foods, a separate unit

Spaghetti Carbonara	Pasta with ham or bacon, eggs, and cream finished with parmesan cheese. Should only be eaten by those unconcerned with weight or cholesterol
Stiff	Person who doesn't tip or is dead (same thing, really)
Supremes	Chicken breast and upper wing, bone out in the breast
Two fingers	Two ounces
Walk-in	A refrigerated room you can walk into
Whites	Kitchen uniforms, chef coats, pants, shirts, and aprons
Wood flour	Ground sawdust used to smoke meats

Daggers and Men's Smiles
A Moretti and Falla Mystery
by Jill Downie
978-1554888689
$11.99

On the English Channel Island of Guernsey, Detective Inspector Ed Moretti and his new partner, Liz Falla, investigate vicious attacks on Epicure Films. The international production company is shooting a movie based on British bad-boy author Gilbert Ensor's bestselling novel about an Italian aristocratic family at the end of the Second World War, using the manor house belonging to the expatriate Vannonis. When vandalism escalates into murder, Moretti must resist the attractions of Ensor's glamorous American wife, Sydney, consolidate his working relationship with Falla, and establish whether the murders on Guernsey go beyond the island.

Lake on the Mountain
A Dan Sharp Mystery
by Jeffrey Round
978-1459700017
$11.99

Dan Sharp, a gay father and missing persons investigator, accepts an invitation to a wedding on a yacht in Ontario's Prince Edward County. It seems just the thing to bring Dan closer to his noncommittal partner, Bill, a respected medical professional with a penchant for sleazy after-hours clubs, cheap drugs, and rough sex. But the event doesn't go exactly as planned.

When a member of the wedding party is swept overboard, a case of mistaken identity leads to confusion as the wrong person is reported missing. The hunt for a possible killer leads Dan deeper into the troubled waters and private lives of a family of rich WASPs and their secret world of privilege. No sooner is that case resolved when a second one ends up on Dan's desk. Dan is hired by an anonymous source to investigate the disappearance twenty years earlier of the groom's father. The only clues are a missing bicycle and six horses mysteriously poisoned.

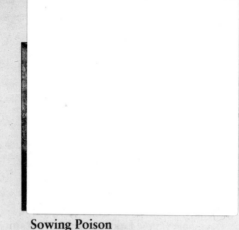

Sowing Poison
A Thaddeus Lewis Mystery
by Janet Kellough
978-1459700543
$11.99

After an absence of many years, Nathan Elliott returns to the lakeside village of Wellington in Ontario's Prince Edward County to be at his dying father's side. Within a few days of his return, his brother, Reuben, reports that Nathan disappeared and no trace of him can be found. Shortly after, Nathan's wife arrives in the village. Claiming that she can contact the dead, she begins to hold séances for the villagers. Thaddeus Lewis, a Methodist circuit rider, is outraged. After coming up against greed, fraud, and murder, can Lewis learn the truth about Nathan Elliott? Religious conflict and political dissension all play a part in this tale set in 1844 Upper Canada.

Available at your favourite bookseller.

DUNDURN
www.dundurn.com

What did you think of this book? Visit *www.dundurn.com* for reviews, videos, updates, and more!